THE
LITTLE
SECRET

THE LITTLE SECRET

Kate Saunders

illustrated by William Carman

FEIWEL and FRIENDS
New York

A Feiwel and Friends Book
An Imprint of Macmillan

Library of Congress Cataloging-in-Publication Data

Saunders, Kate,
The little secret / by Kate Saunders ; illustrated by William Carman.
— 1st ed. p. cm.
Summary: When she is invited to her new friend's home for summer vacation,
eleven-year-old Jane discovers that Staffa and her family are not what they seem
to be.
ISBN: 978-0-312-36961-3
[1. Friendship—Fiction. 2. Kings, queens, rulers, etc.—Fiction.
3. Elves—Fiction. 4. Fantasy.] I. Carman, William, ill. II. Title.
PZ7.S2539Li 2009   [Fic]—dc22   2008034745

First published in the United Kingdom by Macmillan Children's Books,
a division of Pan Macmillan.

Design by Barbara Grzeslo

Feiwel and Friends logo designed by Filomena Tuosto

First U.S. Edition: 2009

10 9 8 7 6 5 4 3 2 1

www.feiwelandfriends.com

For Tom, George, Felix, Elsa, Claudia and Max

With the assistance of Johann Wolfgang von Goethe

This story was inspired by a traveler's tale near
the end of Goethe's novel *Wilhelm Meister's Apprenticeship.*

"Silver Threads Among the Gold,"
by E. E. Rexford and H. P. Danks, 1873

THE NEW GIRL

ON MONDAY MORNING THERE WAS A NEW GIRL IN Jane's class. She stood at the front beside Mrs. Burrows.

"Everyone," said Mrs. Burrows. "This is Staffa. She's spending a few weeks with us until the end of term."

"How do you do," Staffa said.

Everyone stared. Jane thought Staffa was the oddest girl she had ever seen. She must have been eleven, like the rest of the class. But she was as small as an eight-year-old, and very skinny. She had two long braids of shiny black hair. Her skin was paper white, and you could see the blue veins in her spindly little arms. She wore a stiff dress of dark red velvet, white socks and polished black shoes. Jane thought she looked like one of the old-fashioned children in books about the Second World War. Ellie and Angie, the other two girls in the class, had started tittering behind their hands.

Staffa stared right back, not at all shy. She looked carefully at every face in the classroom. This did not take long. Lower Lumpton Primary was a very small school, in a very small town that was really a large village. There were only ten children in the whole of sixth grade.

"Welcome to our school, Staffa," said Mrs. Burrows. "Why don't you tell us something about yourself?"

"There's not much to tell," Staffa said. "I was brought up in a very remote place in the far north. My mother and I are traveling 'round the country, on our annual tour of interesting places. We're resting here for a while, before we make our long journey home, and I'm hoping to make a new best friend."

Staffa's voice was babyish and squeaky, but she spoke like a posh and rather nutty old lady. She sounded hilarious, and the whole class was giggling. Jane tried to keep a straight face because it felt mean to laugh at someone new, but even Mrs. Burrows was smiling.

"Thank you, Staffa. I'm sure you'll make lots of new friends."

"Oh, I'm only looking for one," Staffa said.

The giggles got louder.

"Settle down!" warned Mrs. Burrows.

Staffa did not seem to care about being laughed at. She smiled graciously. "Please don't worry about me, Mrs. Burrows. My life has been rich and varied, and I'm quite used to new experiences. Shall I sit next to that boy with the red hair?"

"Boy with — ? Oh, you mean Jane!"

The class exploded into a roar of laughter.

Jane felt that if she blushed any harder, her ears would catch fire. This weird new girl had mistaken her for a boy and mentioned her hair. She couldn't have said anything worse. The two things Jane hated most about her life were her red hair and the fact that she had to wear boys' clothes.

"Jane's certainly not a boy," Mrs. Burrows said with a kind look at Jane and a stern look at the rest of the class. "I expect you thought she was a boy because she has her lovely hair tied back."

"But she's dressed as a boy," Staffa said. She pointed at Jane's Manchester United sweatshirt. "She's wearing some sort of soccer costume."

There was another burst of laughter. The boys at the back shouted "soccer costume!" in silly posh voices.

Mrs. Burrows told them to be quiet, but she was laughing too. "I don't know where you've been for the past fifty years, Staffa. These days, it's perfectly normal for girls to wear soccer stuff. Look." She put her foot on a chair, hitched up her trouser leg and showed the class her Arsenal sock. "Even old lady teachers do it."

The fire in Jane's face cooled. She was grateful to Mrs. Burrows for taking the attention away from her, but it wasn't much good when the new girl had to sit right beside her. It was the only empty place in the class.

Staffa sat down in the empty place. "Well, this is cozy," she said. She opened an old-fashioned brown leather satchel and began unpacking pencils and paper. "Sorry I thought you were a boy."

"Right, everybody," said Mrs. Burrows. "Let's get started."

"Yes, do carry on," Staffa said. "I'll soon get into the swing of things."

She spoke to Mrs. Burrows like a royal person on an official visit.

Jane wished the new girl had sat somewhere else, but she couldn't help being interested in her. She was tiny and she wore babyish clothes, yet she was not like a child. Staffa filled in her math sheet quickly and neatly. When she handed it in at the end of the lesson, she said, "Forgive the gaps, Mrs. Burrows — long division was always my Achilles' heel."

At break, Staffa sat on the low playground wall. She took a Thermos out of her satchel and poured herself a cup of strong black coffee. Jane thought it smelled disgusting. She was curious. What kind of eleven-year-old drank black coffee?

Ellie and Angie called Jane over to their corner of the playground. Normally, these two spent most of their time whispering together and ignoring Jane. Today, they needed her so they could whisper about Staffa.

Ellie said, "You'd never get me in a dress like that. It looks like curtains."

Angie said, "Her shoes are stupid too — toddler's shoes. And she's got a stupid name."

"I quite like her name," Jane said. She was surprised that she wanted to stick up for the new girl. "It's different."

"Oh, like you've got such great taste," Ellie said scornfully.

"Janey!" Jane's younger brothers, Mike and Phil, yelled at her from the other side of the playground. "Come and play soccer! We need another man!"

Angie giggled. "Does Staffa know you're a girl yet?"

"She thinks you're a red-haired boy," Ellie said. "She probably likes you."

Jane scowled and ran off to play soccer, hating Ellie and Angie. She could swear they got sillier every year. All they talked about was clothes and makeup. If only the new girl had been someone she could talk to sensibly.

But Staffa didn't seem to want to talk at all. She spent the rest of break sipping coffee and looking at her watch. When they returned to the classroom, she yawned and stared out of the window.

At lunchtime, she turned to Jane. "I assume that smell of boiled socks is our midday meal."

This made Jane smile — the school lunch did smell rather like boiled socks. "It's okay when you eat it," she said. "I'll show you where we go." Someone had to look after Staffa.

And I suppose it'll have to be me, Jane thought crossly, because there isn't anyone else — just my luck to get stuck with the oddball.

She led Staffa into the lunch hall. Staffa immediately went over to one of the long tables and sat down.

"Is there a menu?" she asked. "Or does one ask the waiting woman?"

Jane swallowed a snort of laughter. She did not believe this girl — Staffa was lucky nobody else had heard her. "We don't sit down until we've gotten our food," she explained. "We have to line up at the window."

Staffa was fascinated. She loved standing in line. She loved watching the lunch ladies, as they spooned out chicken nuggets, baked beans and mountains of fries. She loved the school fries. "These chipped potatoes are delicious! And how clever to put ketchup bottles next to the knives and forks!"

Jane wondered what kind of school Staffa had come from. It must have been a very fancy school, she thought, if it really did have menus and "waiting women."

"This is a highly efficient way of feeding large numbers of people," piped Staffa. "I must tell my mother. She's always trying to cut costs in the servants' canteen."

Jane wished Staffa would stop talking. Couldn't she see that everyone else at the table was staring, and whispering behind their hands? It was very embarrassing.

When she had finished her fries, Staffa wiped her mouth with a lace handkerchief. She stood up. "Let's have our coffee outside."

Jane said, "Wait — we can't just walk out. We have to take the dirty plates back to the kitchen."

Staffa was surprised. "Really? Don't the servants clear the tables?"

Unfortunately, everyone else around the table heard this.

One of the boys — a very nasty boy named Damian Budge — shouted, "Where d'you think you are — Hogwarts?"

Staffa's pale, chilly blue eyes were serious. "You must be patient with me. I haven't the slightest idea what you're talking about."

"Oh, I'm such a posh cow!" squeaked Damian.

Jane said, "Leave her alone."

"Why d'you care? Are you her boyfriend, or something?"

"It's not her fault she's different," Jane said, scowling at him. "Leave her alone, Budge. She's not doing you any harm."

She stood up, took the plates back to the kitchen and almost dragged Staffa out to the playground.

"Thanks for defending me," Staffa said.

"That's okay. But maybe you should try to be a bit less — I mean, not so . . ." Jane was struggling for the right words.

Staffa smiled. "It's the way I speak, isn't it? Don't

worry, I won't be offended. I can see how kind you are, Jane." Her peaky, china-doll face radiated happiness. "I think you're exactly the friend I've been looking for!"

For the rest of that day, Staffa did not take her eyes off Jane. It is very uncomfortable to be stared at by a person who is right beside you. Every time Jane looked up, there were Staffa's pale eyes, inches from her own. She gave Jane secret smiles, as if the two of them were suddenly the best friends in the world. But Jane was not sure she wanted to be Staffa's best friend. The smiling and the staring were creepy, and she was relieved when it was time to go home.

Jane found her brothers in the crowd around the big gate, cheerfully hitting each other with their backpacks. Mike and Phil were identical twins of eight years old, always easy to spot because of their mops of shaggy white-blond hair.

"Come on," she said. "Let's get out of here." She almost ran through the gate.

"Slow down!" shouted Phil.

Out in the street, Mike tugged at Jane's sleeve. "Why's SHE coming with us?"

Jane turned around, and there was Staffa, right behind her. She suddenly looked particularly small — hardly bigger than the twins — and rather scarily delicate. Jane stopped being annoyed. She couldn't shout at someone who looked as if she could be blown away like a leaf.

She took a deep breath. "Look, Staffa, you've driven me mad all day, and now you're stalking me. Why?"

"I thought I'd walk home with you," Staffa said.

"Don't you have a home of your own?"

"It's a long way away." For a moment, Staffa looked sad. "My mother and I are staying in King's Lumpton." This was the larger town nearby, where there were shops and a weekly market. "Mother won't be back yet. And it's dull to go back to an empty house."

Jane felt sorry for her. "D'you want to come over to my house, then?"

Staffa smiled. "I'd love to."

THE BOY GARDEN

STAFFA AND JANE WALKED IN SILENCE. STAFFA WAS still smiling. Jane was uncomfortable. She had blurted out the invitation before she had time to think about it, and she wished there had been time to prepare her family. The house was such a dump. A posh, tidy sort of girl like Staffa would probably be horrified.

"I should warn you," she said, "it's a bit of a mess."

"My dear Jane," Staffa said. "I'm sure I shall find your home perfectly delightful."

They fell back into silence. Mike and Phil ran ahead, kicking their backpacks like dusty soccer balls.

Jane's family lived in a shabby house, surrounded by shabby fields, at the very edge of the village. You reached it by walking along a lane where there were no houses. As they turned down this lane, Staffa became chatty.

"I'm really very sorry about mistaking you for a boy." She linked arms with Jane. "But why do your parents make you wear boys' clothes?"

"Because I've got six brothers," Jane said.

"Six!" Staffa was intensely interested.

"I'm the only girl. There isn't any money for girls' clothes. I have to wear the boys' hand-me-downs."

"Poor you," Staffa said. "That's not fair. If you were the only boy in a family of girls, they wouldn't send you to school in a dress."

This was a good point, and it made Jane laugh. "What about you?" she asked, liking Staffa more. "Do you have brothers and sisters?"

"One brother," Staffa said.

"Older or younger?"

"Much older." Staffa didn't seem to want to talk about him, but Jane was too curious to stop.

"Is he traveling with you?"

"No. He had to go on army exercises."

"So he's a soldier?"

"No, he's a student. But never mind about him — he's boring." Staffa smiled. "I want to hear about every single one of your brothers. Will I meet them all today?"

"You won't meet Martin," Jane said. "He's the oldest. He's nineteen, and away at college. It's great when he's at home, because he's got a car. Does your brother have a car?"

"Yes, of course." Staffa was starting to sound a little cross. "Go on — tell me about the others."

Jane said, "After Martin there's Dan, who's seventeen. He's in high school. And then there's Jon, who's fifteen. My clothes mostly come down from Jon. They always have patches on the knees."

Staffa asked, "Where do they go to school?"

"They're at the high school in King's Lumpton. That's where I'm going in September." Jane glanced doubtfully at Staffa — so small and strange, so unfitted for life at a large secondary school. "I suppose you'll be going there too."

Staffa shook her head. "Mother and I will be gone by then."

"Oh." Jane couldn't quite bring herself to say it was a pity. She went on quickly, "Anyway, after Jon there's me, and after me there's the twins. And last of all there's little Ted. He's only one and a half."

Staffa half closed her eyes, and murmured, "Martin, Dan, Jon, You, Mike and Phil, little Ted."

"Yes, well done. It takes most people ages to sort us out."

"And do any of them have red hair, like yours?"

"Not like mine." Jane's long hair (which she hated, though her mother thought it beautiful) was a deep, dark red. "The others are brown or blond. Little Ted's is sort of orange, like a marmalade-colored cat."

"Oh, Jane, I was so lucky to find you!" Staffa sighed. "I've never had a best friend before."

"Hang on!" This was going too fast. Jane wasn't even sure she liked Staffa. "We can't be best friends yet — it takes time."

"You obviously need a female friend," Staffa said. "Those two silly girls in your class can't possibly satisfy a mind like yours."

They reached the front gate of Jane's house. "Well, here it is," she said. "Welcome to Pike Lane Farm. It's not really a farm — we only have the yard and the paddock. My mom calls it the Boy Garden. She says it's like a bear garden, only noisier."

"What's a bear garden?"

"I don't really know. I think it's just any place that's full of wild beasts."

Staffa chuckled. Her pointed little face sharpened with interest. She looked at the shabby house. She looked at the front yard, which was full of bikes and homemade wooden ramps. She looked at the old, serious horse who stood by the paddock fence.

"The horse is called Leonard," Jane said. "Even the animals here are boys."

The front door was open. The jerseys and backpacks of the twins lay in a heap on the doormat. Jane kicked the heap aside and led Staffa to the kitchen. As usual, the place was a cheerful mess.

Jane's mother was sitting at the kitchen table, feeding little Ted. Jane tried to imagine how they might look to someone posh. Mom's tracksuit was old and baggy. Her hair was tied back with a pair of tights. Little Ted's sweet, pudgy face was covered with stripes of purple marker. He shouted when he saw Jane, and banged his wooden hammer on the tray of his high chair.

Jane laughed. She kissed the top of his head. His marmalade-colored hair was blobbed with tomato sauce. "What've you done to your face, Mr. Silly?"

"He somehow got hold of a purple pen," Jane's mom said. "I turned my back for one moment, and the next thing I knew he was covered with it. It won't wash off, so we'd better get used to it."

Jane looked back at Staffa, wondering if she was shocked by this sordid scene. Staffa was certainly surprised, but she was also smiling. For the first time that day, she looked like a real child. Jane saw that she loved the Boy Garden, and had another moment of liking her.

"Mom," she said, "this is Staffa. She's come to play, if that's okay."

Mom smiled. " 'Course it's okay — you know I'm always glad to see another girl. Hi, Staffa."

"How do you do, Mrs. Hughes," said Staffa. "It's very nice to meet you."

"Janey, get some toast and chocolate cookies, just for yourself and Staffa. I'll feed the rabble when little Ted's finished."

Staffa ate her toast next to little Ted. She watched him with fascination. He smacked her face with his fat wet hand, but she only laughed. Little Ted kindly offered her his soggy crusts, and she pretended to eat them. Every now and then, she said shyly to Mom, "He's so sweet!"

The peace did not last for long. Mike and Phil ran into the kitchen, shouting for juice and cookies. The front door slammed. Dan and Jon came in from their school. They were both taller than Mom, with deep voices you could feel in the floor. The room was suddenly bursting

with people. Jane was worried that Staffa would feel over-
whelmed, but she was still smiling. She was not at all shy
with the big boys, and she jumped up eagerly when Dan
suggested they should go out into the backyard.

The sunny afternoon was beginning to fade. There
was a pleasant breeze. Mike and Phil practiced skateboard-
ing on the long concrete path. Dan and Jon raced up and
down the homemade ramps on their bikes. Jane offered
to lend Staffa Phil's bike, not really thinking she would
accept — but Staffa surprised her by flinging herself at
it and charging up the ramps like a red velvet whirlwind.
Jane leapt on her own bike (outgrown by Jon) and charged
after her.

They had a great time racing girls against boys. Staffa
was no longer shy, and not at all delicate. She yelled orders, she threw clumps of dirt at the boys, she invented
daring and dangerous challenges. Dan and Jon thought
Staffa was hilarious. The two teams battled for possession
of the garden hose. The boys won, and sprayed Staffa and
Jane with cold water.

By the end of the afternoon, Jane had laughed
and screamed so much that her stomach muscles ached.
She was soaked with water and streaked with dirt. One of
Staffa's velvet sleeves was torn. They lay down on the rough

grass, gasping for breath. The sun was lower down in the sky now. Little Ted, playing in his sandbox by the back door, cast a long, spidery shadow.

Staffa sighed. "It's getting late. I'd better go home."

They sat up, giggling again at the state of their clothes.

Jane asked, "How will you get there? My dad's got the car, so we can't give you a lift, and there aren't any buses."

"Don't worry, I'll call our driver."

"Your what?"

Staffa stood up, brushing dirt from her dress. "Our driver. He waits for me after school."

Once again, she was cool and solemn. She fetched her satchel. She thanked Mom for a lovely afternoon. She kissed little Ted — adding sand to the dirt on her dress. From her satchel she took a flashy cellphone. She pressed a single button and made one short call.

Jane walked with her down the long lane. They were dreamily silent for a minute, until Staffa said, "Jane, I haven't had so much fun in years."

"You sound like my grandma."

"Seriously, it's been a wonderful afternoon. The whole day has been wonderful."

A huge, shining black car had stopped at the end of the lane. It was the kind of car that the Queen rides in when she doesn't want anyone to see her. The back windows were dark. A driver sat very still in the front seat. He (or she) wore a peaked cap, pulled very low. In spite of the warm weather, he (or she) was muffled in miles and miles of black scarf.

Staffa squeezed Jane's hand. "I don't need to look for a best friend anymore. I've found you."

LADY MATILDA

IT CAME AS A SHOCK THE NEXT DAY, TO REMEMBER HOW peculiar Staffa looked beside the rest of the class. Her braids were so black and stiff, and had a shine that made Jane think of plastic. This time, instead of the red-velvet dress, Staffa was wearing a pleated skirt of navy blue, with straps over the shoulders and a starched white blouse. This outfit sent Ellie and Angie into fits of giggles.

Staffa didn't seem to care about the giggling, but it made her thoughtful. At break, she pulled Jane over to the low wall in the playground.

"Would you like a cup of coffee?"

"No thanks." Jane did not sit down beside her. She wasn't nearly as sure as Staffa that the two of them were "best friends."

Staffa calmly opened her Thermos and poured herself a cup of black coffee. Again, the bitter smell of it made Jane wrinkle her nose.

"I can't help noticing," Staffa said, "that my clothes are attracting attention. There must be something wrong with them."

Jane was embarrassed. "Well — "

"Please tell me the truth, Jane. It's important that I blend in. What's wrong with my clothes?"

"They're just a bit — fancy."

Staffa nodded, not at all offended. "And perhaps a little out of date?"

"Er — maybe."

"I must buy some new things. I need some pants, like yours. I could have beaten Dan and Jon yesterday if I'd been able to move properly."

Jane laughed. "That'd serve them right — I'd love to beat those two."

"And I had a very good idea last night, Jane. We should build an army assault course in your paddock — I know all about them, because of my brother's experiences in the army. Those old oil drums would make an excellent tunnel."

Jane was impressed. This was a terrific idea. She could hardly wait to tell Dan and Jon. "Yes, and there's loads of ropes and stuff in the garage. I'll ask my dad what we can have. Can you come over again after school?"

"Actually, I was rather hoping you'd come home with me. I'd like you to meet my mother."

"Oh." Jane tried to picture what the mother of Staffa could be like. She was curious, and a little scared. "Okay."

She could not have escaped, even if she had wanted to. The moment school was over, Staffa took her hand. She marched over to the gate, where Mike and Phil were waiting.

"Please tell Mrs. Hughes that Jane's coming to tea with me today. We'll bring her home at about half past six."

Jane never went to tea with anyone, and it felt strange to see the twins walking away from her. Staffa tugged her in the opposite direction. The huge black car was parked around the corner, in a narrow side street next to the convenience store. The same driver, wrapped in a black scarf that covered his (or her) face, sat behind the wheel as still as a statue. Staffa opened the door. Jane climbed in after her, very conscious of her extremely muddy sneakers. The inside of the car was very grand and spotlessly clean. The seats were made of the softest leather, and there were all sorts of little cupboards and compartments.

A sheet of glass separated them from the driver. Staffa picked up a long tube and spoke into a kind of metal bulb at the top. "Market Square, please."

The engine purred. The car pulled away. Staffa opened one of the little doors.

"Wow," Jane said. "You've got a fridge!"

The fridge was crammed with cans and bottles. Staffa took out two cans of cola. "Yes, it's a convenient car for people who do a lot of traveling."

Jane sipped cola and leaned more comfortably against the seat. Though the windows of the car looked black on the outside, you could see out of them perfectly normally. She found that she was enjoying the smooth, luxurious ride. Wait till her brothers heard about this.

"Your parents must be very rich," she said.

"My mother is, I suppose," Staffa said. "My father's dead."

"Oh — sorry." The little worm of envy that had begun to nibble at Jane quickly died. "That's awful."

Staffa shrugged. "He died when I was a baby. To tell the truth, we don't miss him much."

Jane was shocked. If anything had happened to her dad, the whole family would have been brokenhearted.

Staffa saw the look on her face, and smiled. "So you see, we're only rich in money. In every other sense, you're the rich one."

She looked so pale and sad that Jane felt ashamed of envying her. All the money in the world couldn't buy a Boy Garden.

Staffa opened another little door. There was a television behind it. Staffa turned it on, and the two of them swished into King's Lumpton while watching the news. The car halted in the empty market square.

"I told Mother all about you," Staffa said. "She can't wait to meet you. Please don't be shy." They got out of the car. "We're staying at the Crown and Sceptre."

"Oh," Jane said. It came out as a squeak. The Crown and Sceptre was the town's only fancy hotel. It had a famous French wine list and took up one whole side of the square. Jane had never been inside. She had only seen the polished wooden doors, and the lamps at the windows. She felt very shabby in her jeans and T-shirt.

Staffa strolled into the lobby as if she owned the place.

The carpet was deep and squashy. There were lots of sofas, and palm trees in brass tubs. A lady was playing the harp while other ladies had tea very quietly. Jane scuttled after Staffa, hoping nobody was looking at her.

In the elevator, on the way up, Staffa suddenly said, "By the way, you have to call my mother Lady Matilda. She goes mad if you don't."

"Lady Matilda," Jane repeated. She had never met anyone with a title. The idea was partly scary, and partly silly.

"But please don't be nervous. She's really all right when you get to know her."

The elevator took them to a corridor, full of hush and polish.

Staffa opened a door. "Sorry we're late," she said. "Here she is."

"Well, well," said a deep, rich, plummy voice. "So this is your friend Jane."

Jane, feeling that her flaming face was as red as her hair, mumbled, "How do you do — er — Lady Matilda."

"Oh, this is very good," said Lady Matilda. "Very good indeed. Well done, Staffa."

Staffa's mother sat on a velvet chair that was a kind of throne. She was a large lady, with a steep slope of a bosom. Her hair was like Staffa's — black and glossy and curiously lifeless. Her wide lips were painted bright red. She wore a long gown of bright blue satin. It was hard to tell how old she was. She looked older than Jane's mom, yet there was not a line on her white skin. Lady Matilda's skin was dead white. So were her large teeth, but it was a flat sort of whiteness, that reminded Jane of bathrooms.

"I'm thrilled to meet you, Jane." Lady Matilda held out her hand. Her large fingers sparkled with jewels. Jane managed to shake hands, still blushing furiously.

"Sit down. Staffa will make us some tea. What kind of tea do you like, Jane? I can offer Assam, or Darjeeling — or my own particular favorite, a tea made from the bitter Haw-haw, which grows only in the gardens of my mountain home."

"Mother, don't be silly," Staffa said. "It's too hot for tea. We'll have fruit juice."

"Oh, suit yourselves." Lady Matilda's glassy blue eyes flickered with annoyance. "You can make me a cup of Haw-haw with six sugars." Her huge red-and-white smile snapped back. "What wonderful hair you have, Jane — why, you're quite a beauty! How stupendous you'd look in a lime green ball gown!"

Staffa said, "Really? I see her more in bright blue."

"Oh no, dear — such an unforgiving shade! Kingfisher, perhaps."

Nobody had ever discussed what kind of ball gown Jane should wear. Feeling very shy, but also rather pleased, she sat down in the armchair opposite Lady Matilda. Staffa gave her a glass of cool, sweet mango juice. She lit a gaslight under a large brass kettle, which hung on a special little stand on the low table.

"Staffa has told me about your home," Lady Matilda said. "Six brothers! What does your father do, my dear?"

Jane told her that her dad was a postman, who also worked some evenings at the local pub and did people's gardening. He was a popular figure in Lower Lumpton, and she was pleased when Lady Matilda said he sounded like a "splendid fellow."

Staffa went into another room and came back pushing a large trolley. It was laden, top and bottom, with the most incredible afternoon tea — toast and crumpets on special hot dishes, plates of cream cakes, jam tarts and chocolate meringues. Jane began to relax. Lady Matilda was very kind and flattering, and she told Jane to eat as much as she wanted. Jane ate the delicious cakes, trying not to answer Lady Matilda's questions with her mouth full.

Lady Matilda seemed to have a great fondness for sugar. Her big white teeth chomped pastries and custards and chocolate creams in a way that made Jane think of Leonard the horse. When she saw that her nosiness was making Jane uncomfortable, Lady Matilda stopped asking questions. Sipping purple Haw-haw tea from a cup the size of a soup bowl, she began to tell fantastic stories, all about the northern land where she and Staffa lived. She described winter skating parties, summer balls that lasted all night, and water carnivals on the lake beside her mountain castle. It sounded wonderful.

Could it possibly be true? Jane noticed that some of the stories made Staffa frown. Perhaps she was embarrassed because her mother was making things up.

On the other hand, it was obvious that Lady Matilda and Staffa came from nowhere ordinary. Jane couldn't have said exactly why or how, but she knew they were not ordinary people. It was quite easy to imagine them dancing through the night in grand ballrooms, wearing silks dyed to look like the wings of butterflies.

"All this talk of dancing makes me thirsty," said Lady Matilda. "I need another cup of tea." She held out her enormous cup.

Staffa (who wasn't eating anything) took the cup. She filled it from the huge, pear-shaped brass teapot. There was a strong smell of orange peel and gasoline. The tea was such a dark purple that it looked almost black.

Jane was looking curiously around the room. Most of the furniture was comfortable and boring, and obviously belonged to the hotel. But Lady Matilda's throne-like chair was surrounded by all kinds of strange objects, which she must have brought from her home. On the low table, beside the big brass teapot, there was a large picture in a gold frame, of a handsome young man in some kind of uniform — Jane wondered if he was Staffa's brother. Next to the picture was a huge and hideous brass spider, upon which was carved the word "Tornado."

The strangest and most beautiful thing in the room was a box that stood on a table at her ladyship's side. It was about the size of a small bedside cabinet, perfectly square and covered all over with paintings so wonderful that Jane felt she could have stared at them forever — castles, mountains, deep forests bathed in sunlight. The colors were so rich and bright that it almost hurt to look at them.

Lady Matilda smiled broadly (with her mouth full of doughnut). "Ah, you're looking at my box. Do you like it?"

Jane said, truthfully, "I think it's the most beautiful thing I've ever seen."

"What good taste you have," Lady Matilda said. "It's an old family treasure, made by our people many hundreds of years ago. I simply can't travel without it. I must have my comforts around me. My gold teapot, for instance — you must always brew Haw-haw in a teapot of solid gold."

"Gold?" Jane was fascinated. "I thought it was made of brass!"

"Certainly not — that would ruin the flavor."

Jane saw now that the yellow metal of the teapot was far too beautiful to be brass. She tried to remember whether solid gold was softer or harder than brass. Wouldn't the flame of the gaslight melt it? She decided to ask Mom, who was good at science. "What about the spider?" she asked. "Is that solid gold too?"

Lady Matilda patted the large and hideous spider. "Oh, yes. Only gold was good enough for him." She leaned across the table. "His name was Tornado. He was a racing spider. I had this little statue made when he won the Queen's Cup for the tenth time."

"Oh," Jane said. She had not known there was any such thing as a racing spider.

"Poor Tornado died shortly afterwards," Lady Matilda said. "Four of his legs were broken. He had to be shot."

"Oh." Jane looked uneasily at Staffa. This sounded crazy. What kind of gun would be tiny enough to shoot a spider? Wouldn't it have been simpler just to step on it?

Staffa jumped up. "I think Jane has to go home now."

"Oh, what a shame," said Lady Matilda. "It's been a delight to meet you, Jane." She rose from her throne. She was very tall, and she loomed over Jane like a great blue satin cliff. "Staffa, find a big bag and fill it up with cakes for Jane's brothers."

"Good idea," said Staffa. "And can I go to have tea at the Boy Garden tomorrow?"

"Yes, dear. I don't see why not."

"You like Jane, don't you?"

Lady Matilda smiled. "She's perfect!"

Jane was puzzled. Why were Staffa and her mother nodding at each other in that odd way? The strong smell of the Haw-haw tea was starting to make her a little dizzy. She was glad it was time to go home.

Staffa went into the other room to fetch the cakes. Lady Matilda bent down towards Jane. "Next time you come, my dear child," she said, "I'll show you some pictures of ball dresses. And I might measure your head for a crown."

"A — what?" Now Jane knew she had to be crazy.

"Don't be alarmed, Jane. It's just a little game I like to play! Just a game!"

Staffa came back, holding a large shopping bag. Jane

jumped up and stammered out her thanks. It was a relief to leave the hot, perfumed room.

Jane and Staffa took the elevator downstairs. Outside the hotel entrance, the big car was waiting.

"Here." Staffa handed the bag to Jane.

"Oh, wow!" It was stuffed with the most glorious cakes — more than enough for even the greedy Boy Garden. "Staffa, thanks so much!"

"I hope you won't mind going in the car by yourself. The driver knows where to go."

"I don't mind," Jane said, though she did mind a bit — the muffled driver gave her the creeps.

"Don't try to talk to him," Staffa said. "He can't hear you unless you speak through the tube. Hope the boys like the cakes."

Suddenly, without warning, she gave Jane a quick hug and ran back into the hotel.

Jane lay back against the soft leather seats of the fabulous car, feeling like a film star — wouldn't the boys go crazy when they saw her getting out? This had been an incredible afternoon. Her head was spinning with all the wonderful things she had seen and heard — the gold spider, the painted box, the purple tea, the stories of castles and all-night parties. Staffa and her mother had said some very odd things, she thought. What was all that about Jane being "perfect"? And why did Lady Matilda want to measure her head for a crown?

Jane decided not to tell her parents too much about the visit. She was afraid she would make Staffa's mother sound absolutely crazy. They might stop her from going back, and she couldn't bear that. She hadn't seen nearly enough.

AN INVITATION

Over the next few weeks — slightly to Jane's surprise — she and Staffa gradually turned into real best friends. Staffa's plan to build an army assault course took the Boy Garden by storm. Jane and Staffa and all the boys except little Ted worked on it every day after school, and most weekends, and the shabby paddock was soon a forest of ropes, ladders and oil-drum tunnels. Leonard the horse was moved into the next field, and watched them over the fence with polite interest.

Jane had never had a close friend who was a girl, and as the weeks of the school year went by, she found that she liked Staffa more and more. The peculiar little creature spoke like a nutty old lady, and her clothes never did look normal, but she could race around the assault course like a monkey and she was great at thinking up dangerous games. All the boys thought she was a terrific laugh.

Staffa was extremely generous. She gave them a real climbing net, to make a Wall of Death on the assault course. She gave Jane a three-pack of lovely flowered socks. She gave little Ted a toy fire engine, and her mysterious driver often bought bags of cakes and sweets.

"You mustn't spend all this money on us, Staffa," Jane's mom said. "We don't charge an entrance fee — we'll be happy if you just bring yourself."

Staffa said, very seriously, "Please, Mrs. Hughes, grant me this indulgence. My mother and I have more money than we know what to do with. And it isn't often used to bring people pleasure."

"Poor little kid," Jane's dad said later. "All she wants is a real family." He told Jane that Staffa was always more than welcome at the Boy Garden.

Once a week, Staffa took Jane for tea with Lady Matilda. Jane enjoyed these stuffy, strange afternoons. There were always amazing cakes, and large bowls of Woolworth's Pick-and-Mix. Lady Matilda told more fantastic stories about her mountain castle. "Well, it's more of a hunting lodge, really — much smaller and cozier than my main castle in the city. I often send my servants there when they're ill."

Jane noticed that Staffa was irritated when her mother talked about the hunting lodge, and wondered why. Though she made such a racket while at the Boy Garden, Staffa was usually very quiet during these afternoons. She obeyed her mother's orders like a servant, leaping up to make her endless cups of purple, gasoline-smelling Hawhaw tea.

Lady Matilda talked about ball dresses and hats and jewels, and Jane pretended to listen while she stared at the painted box. The colors of the box were so vivid, and the paintings were so realistic, that she could have sworn they were a little different each time she saw them — had there always been a sunset behind those trees? Wasn't that a new cloud beside the castle turret? She didn't think she could ever get tired of looking.

One thing bothered her. Lady Matilda's stories gradually became more and more far-fetched.

"Oh, I wish you could see our Winter Sleigh Race, Jane! When the ice on the great mountain lake is so thick that you can build a bonfire on it! That's where we hold the Skating Ball, and I hand out prizes for the fastest!

And the ice boxing is very exciting too — but my favorite occasion is the Spring Flower Fight, when you can hardly see for the blizzard of petals!"

It was all fascinating, but how much of it was true? Jane waited for a chance to ask Staffa without hurting her feelings. It came one sunny afternoon, a couple of weeks before the end of term. Staffa and Jane were in the paddock, sunbathing against the Wall of Death.

"I must say, I admire you for being so patient with Mother," Staffa said. "She can be such a crashing bore sometimes."

"She does go on a bit," Jane admitted. "Specially when she starts talking about correct behavior, and curtseying to people, and stuff. But I love hearing all the stories about your home. Is it — is it all true? You know, the castles, and the ice balls, and the midnight picnics — "

Staffa laughed, rather grimly. "Oh, those bits are all perfectly true."

"Are any bits not true? Which bits?"

"I can't explain." Staffa was unhappy.

"Why not?"

"It would take too long."

"We're supposed to be best friends," Jane reminded her. "You should be able to tell me anything."

Staffa looked at her in silence for a long time. She shook her head. "It's too complicated."

A very loud blast on a car horn made them both jump. A huge black car raced up the lane, and halted outside the front gate.

"Good grief," Staffa said. "It's Mother!"

"You're joking!" Jane was horrified — what on earth would Lady Matilda think of the mad, messy Boy Garden?

"Don't panic." Staffa stood up briskly. "I'll try to stop her from being too embarrassing."

The car door opened, and out climbed Lady Matilda. "Coo-ee, little girls!" she called. "Isn't this a surprise? I've come to call on Jane's parents! I wanted to see those shining honest faces for myself!"

She was wearing a huge pair of tweed knickerbockers, as baggy as Victorian bloomers. They were teamed with a matching tweed jacket, squeezed very tight over her steep bosom, and tight purple boots with high heels.

"I thought I'd better dress down," said Lady Matilda. "Jane's family will be very simple folk, and I want to put them at their ease."

Dan, Jon and the twins had rushed out of the house to stare at the gleaming car. They stared even harder when they saw Staffa's mother. Jane had told them very little about Lady Matilda, mainly because she didn't think anyone would believe her.

Lady Matilda gave them a gracious wave. "What handsome brothers you have, Jane." She pointed to Mom and Dad, who were standing at the door with little Ted. "And I suppose these two humble peasants are your parents?"

Staffa's white cheeks turned pink. "They're not peasants!" she hissed.

Dad obviously wanted to laugh, but was too kind. "How do you do, Lady Matilda. Welcome to our humble home." He gave the girls a friendly wink. "Please come inside and have a cup of tea."

Mom picked up little Ted, just in time to stop him from grabbing Lady Matilda's tweed bloomers with his very dirty hand. "It's lovely to meet you at last — now we can thank you for all the presents."

"My dear Mrs. Hughes, please don't thank me!" cried Lady Matilda. "It was the least I could do!"

She strode into the house. Mom and Dad hurried after her.

"Sorry about the chaos," Dad said.

Lady Matilda did not seem to notice the eggy plates and piles of crumbs, or the crowd of boys' faces staring at her from the doorway. She sat down on the strongest-looking chair, which creaked under her weight, and almost disap-peared between the cheeks of her bloomered bottom.

"I have come with an invitation," she said. "In the few weeks that Staffa and I have known your daughter Jane, we have grown very fond of her. She is such a treasure — so delicate and refined!"

The boys snorted with laughter. Mom made a warning face at them.

"My daughter and I will soon be leaving this part of the country," said Lady Matilda. "And we would very much like to take Jane back to our home, for a short holiday."

"Oh, yes!" Staffa cried. "Please say you'll come, Jane!"

"I — I don't know — " Jane was bewildered. She had never been away from her home, unless you counted the family camping trips at the seaside. She had never been separated from her family, and the prospect was a little scary. But it was a dazzling offer — to see, with her own eyes, the fabulous lakes, castles and mountains of Lady Matilda's stories.

Lady Matilda smiled her big, rather cold red-and-white smile. "Just for a few weeks, at the beginning of the long summer vacation. We will travel in my car, and I hope we'll be able to buy Jane some new clothes that are actually designed for girls — well, she'll need some, for her new school."

Mom and Dad looked at each other. Jane knew they wanted her to start at King's Lumpton High with proper girls' clothes, and were worried about finding the money.

"It's really kind of you," Mom began, "but we couldn't — "

"You would be doing me a great favor, Mrs. Hughes," Lady Matilda said. "Poor Staffa gets so lonely — don't you, dear?"

"Nothing's any fun when you're on your own." Staffa said. "Do say yes, Jane — there's so much I'd like to show you!"

"Our country home is a very healthy place," Lady Matilda went on. "But the communications are primitive. You mustn't worry if Jane can't speak to you on the telephone. She can keep in touch with postcards, which were always good enough in my day. And I promise — I absolutely promise — to treat her like my very own daughter. She will live like a princess, which is nothing less than she deserves." She leaned forward. The chair cracked alarmingly. "What do you think, Mr. Hughes?"

"Well," Dad said, "I've no objection — but it's really up to Jane. Would you like to go, darling?"

Jane said, "I'd totally love to."

Staffa gave a shriek of joy. She gave Jane a hug so hard that it almost hurt, and whispered fiercely in her ear, "You won't be sorry you did this!"

TRAVELS WITH A BOX

THEY SET OUT ON THE VERY FIRST DAY OF THE SUMMER
vacation. Lady Matilda had told Jane not to bring too much
luggage, so she had stuffed just a few belongings into her
school backpack — a book, a toothbrush, a hairbrush, and
a single change of clothes.

The car arrived at the Boy Garden right after breakfast. Lady Matilda leapt out, dressed in a trouser suit of
bright-orange velvet and a matching hat like an orange-
velvet crash helmet. "The open road beckons!" she cried.
"Say your farewells, dear girls!"

The morning was bright and sunny, and Jane was

excited. Much as she loved the Boy Garden, she longed to see new sights and have new experiences. "I'll send loads of postcards," she promised her brothers. "I'll have a lot to tell when I get home!"

"Bring sweets!" shouted Mike and Phil.

Staffa's good-byes took longest. She kissed all the boys — including the oldest, Martin, who had only just gotten back from college. She kissed Mom and Dad, and thanked them for their kindness.

"Oh, do hurry up!" Lady Matilda said crossly. "Kissing them all takes so LONG!"

Staffa gave one last hug and kiss to little Ted. She climbed into the car beside Jane. As they moved away, Jane saw tears on her white cheeks. It was the first time she had ever seen Staffa crying. She took her hand.

"Staffa? Are you okay?"

"I'll miss them, that's all." Staffa did her best to smile. "I've had the time of my life at your Boy Garden. I'm glad I'm taking you away with me, as a souvenir." She added, "For a few weeks, anyway. I don't think I could bear it otherwise."

"Oh, for goodness sake," said Lady Matilda. "Don't be such a drip."

Jane thought this was mean of her. She gave Staffa's

hand a friendly squeeze. "You can come back whenever you like."

"No, I can't," Staffa said. "I can't do anything I like."

It was an odd remark, which made her mother scowl. When Lady Matilda frowned, deep furrows appeared in her white forehead, and she looked like the painted figurehead of an old-fashioned ship. Jane was a little afraid of her.

"Staffa, I'm warning you now — I will not put up with sulking. Make me a cup of Haw-haw tea."

"Yes, Mother."

"And only four sugars, because I've decided to make my bottom smaller. I couldn't get my knickerbockers over it this morning."

"Yes, Mother." Staffa gave a snort of laughter, and winked at Jane to tell her she was all right.

The big gold teapot, complete with gaslight, was traveling with them in the car. So was the painted box. This beautiful object sat on the leather seat between Staffa and her mother, held perfectly still with its own seat belt. Lady Matilda often stroked it, and rested her jeweled hand upon it. Every now and then she wiped it with a silk handkerchief, though there was never a speck on its painted sides. She covered it carefully with the handkerchief while she drank her tea.

They stopped for lunch at a large hotel, somewhere in the middle of the countryside. It was very grand. Lady Matilda begged Jane to order whatever she fancied, and she chose a fancy kind of sausage and mashed potatoes, with ice cream to follow. It was all delicious.

"I MUST get you some new clothes, Jane," Lady Matilda said, looking scornfully at Jane's jeans and sneakers. "Really, you look as if you'd come to mend the boiler!" She frowned down at her menu. "What a miserable selection of puddings! It's a good thing I'm on a diet — I'll just have two of each."

Staffa, who had cheered up, gave Jane a nudge under the table. She nodded towards a painting on the wall of a large pig, and then nodded towards her greedy mother. Both girls shook with secret giggles. Jane knew this was rude, but she couldn't help it — Lady Matilda's big, gobbling red mouth looked so funny with the orange helmet.

After lunch, there was more driving. The car stopped in the busy main street of a large town.

Lady Matilda reached into a kind of pouch that was sewn into the leather of the seat, and pulled out a thick pile of cash. Jane was astonished. It was the most money she had ever seen in real life.

Staffa saw the way Jane stared at it. "Cash is very convenient," she said, "when you travel as much as we do."

"Come along, girlies!" sang Lady Matilda.

They got out of the car. Jane saw that the mysterious driver stayed stock still in the front seat, like a statue wrapped in black.

"What about him?" she asked. "Isn't he getting out too?"

"Who?" Lady Matilda asked vaguely, "Oh, you mean Prockwald."

This was the first time Jane had heard the driver's name. She felt unkind for not asking about it sooner. "Doesn't Mr. Prockwald want to come with us?"

Lady Matilda gave a loud gasp — scaring off a nearby flock of pigeons — and burst into hoots of deafening laughter. Her dull, white teeth opened and shut like a poacher's trap. "Jane, you're too priceless! Staffa, did you ever? MISTER Prockwald!"

Bewildered, Jane looked at Staffa. What had she said that was so hilarious?

"He's a servant," Staffa explained. She was embarrassed. "They're — not like us."

"Why not?"

"You must understand, my dear Jane," said Lady

Matilda, "that these people don't have our fine feelings, or our exquisite tastes. It's unkind to pay them too much attention — it only confuses them. I promise you, Prockwald will be perfectly happy to wait in the car."

Jane had never heard anyone speak in such a heartless, nasty way — though Prockwald didn't seem to mind. She thought how angry her dad would be, if he caught someone talking like that in the pub.

"Anyway," her ladyship went on, "he has to stay here, to guard the box." She took one last, loving look at the beautiful painted box before she shut the car door.

With her mountainous orange bosom leading the way, Lady Matilda took the two girls into a famous shop, full of lovely clothes.

The next half hour was like a daydream. Jane had often thought how great it would be to go into a shop and buy every single thing she wanted. This was exactly what Lady Matilda did. She whisked through the rails of clothes, scooping up skirts, dresses, tops, shoes and bags, until Jane felt slightly giddy — were all these things for her? The clothes were rather girly, and some of the colors (sugary mauve, neon yellow) were rather "bleck," but Jane couldn't say anything without seeming ungrateful. For the first time in her life, she would be totally dressed as a girl. It was incredible, and she was not going to argue about a few colors.

Lady Matilda surprised the girl at the register by handing over the whole heap of money. "You count it out, dear — I can't be bothered." She let out a sigh. "Really, what an appalling place! No junior debutante evening gowns! No dancing pumps! And absolutely NO semiformal cocktail dresses in children's sizes! This is what happens when girls stop wearing corsets. Oh, well."

Festooned with plastic bags, she led Staffa and Jane out of the shop. Prockwald waited beside the car.

Lady Matilda dropped the bags in a heap at his feet. "Put these in the trunk, then drive us to the hotel — and I'll be drinking tea back there, so take the corners slowly."

Staffa brewed another pot of the purple Haw-haw tea. The car filled up with a smell of gasoline and orange peel. Lady Matilda drank two cups and fell asleep.

"That's the one good thing about this revolting tea," said Staffa, switching on the television. "It's like her having an off button."

Jane settled back against the soft leather seat. She was having such a fantastic time, she could hardly believe it was real. The posh car, the new clothes, the wonderful food — she couldn't wait to tell the boys. This was the vacation of her dreams.

Their hotel was an old manor house, in the middle of

the countryside. At the reception desk in the hall, Jane learned that she was to have her own bedroom and bathroom, with cable television and a mini-bar full of sweets. It was so thrilling that she hardly noticed the oddity of Lady Matilda's arrangements.

"So that's one room with bath for Miss Hughes, one large double with bath for myself and my daughter, one single for my driver (though I still don't see why he can't sleep in the corridor), and one room for my box. Prockwald, bring Miss Jane's new clothes. I will carry the box myself."

Lady Matilda went upstairs, holding the painted box carefully in her gloved hands.

"The box first," she said. "Staffa, unlock the door of twenty-two."

Staffa was carrying the keys to all their rooms. She opened the door of number 22. Lady Matilda carried the box inside and placed it carefully on the dressing table. Staffa took two gold candlesticks out of a special canvas case she was carrying, and Lady Matilda placed these on either side of the box. Jane watched, completely baffled. What on earth were they doing?

Strangest of all, the box apparently had a room to itself. Lady Matilda locked the door and put the key in her pocket.

"Staffa, dear, you and I are next door. Jane, you're

across the way. Do have all the sweets you like, and please put on the flowered green dress for dinner. I will see you in the dining room in precisely forty-five minutes."

Staffa handed her the key. Jane let herself into her room. It was wonderful. There was a huge bed, a fridge filled with sweets and a shining bathroom with tiny bottles of shower gel and shampoo. There was a telephone beside the bed. Jane looked up the instructions for making a call, and called the Boy Garden.

Mom answered the phone, and Jane had a sudden attack of homesickness. She could hear little Ted squawking in the background, and Dad having some sort of argument with Jon. For a moment, she longed for the messy kitchen, and the small television, and the big sofa with the stuffing leaking out.

She cheered up when she started telling Mom about her luxury lifestyle, and the heaps of new clothes.

"How generous of Staffa's mother!" Mom said. "Please say thanks from us."

Jane said, "I miss you a lot."

"We miss you too, darling. But we all want you to go on having a lovely time."

The phone call ended with all the boys shouting, " 'Bye Jane!"

The luxurious room felt too quiet after that. Jane distracted herself by finding the flowered green dress and putting it on. There were white tights and green shoes to go with it. Jane stared at herself in the mirror. Anybody could see that she was not a boy. She was a girl, and when she wore girl's clothes, she was actually pretty.

Feeling very elegant but rather shy, Jane made her way downstairs to the hotel dining room. Lady Matilda had booked a private room, which had a view of a garden and a round table with a white cloth.

"My dear Jane," Staffa said, "you look delightful." She was alone.

Jane asked, "Where's Lady Matilda?"

For a moment, Staffa was uncomfortable. "Oh — she said we should start without her. She's — she's been delayed."

"Delayed?"

"I mean, she's doing some business stuff upstairs, and she'll join us when she can."

They were halfway through their bowls of tomato soup when Lady Matilda came crashing into the room.

"So sorry, girlies — I had to catch up with a little paperwork."

Jane stared. Lady Matilda did not look as if she had

been catching up with "paperwork." Her orange suit was speckled with black stuff, like soot, and there was black smoke around her head.

Staffa said, "Your hat's on fire." She picked up her glass of water and poured it on her mother's terrible orange hat.

"Oh, thank you, dear," Lady Matilda said breathlessly. "It must have caught during the explosion — but it's all fine for the time being, and I got two of them with my own hands. Shoot them first, that's what I say — then you won't have the expense of hanging them later."

"Mother," Staffa said softly. She nodded towards Jane.

"Ah," said Lady Matilda. She looked worried for a moment, then gave Jane one of her gleaming, toothy grins. "Don't take any notice, Jane — it's really not important. Someone get me a cup of tea."

What on earth had she been up to? What kind of "explosion" happened in the bedroom of a quiet country hotel? And why was Lady Matilda talking about shooting and hanging? Jane saw the warning looks Staffa was giving to her mother. There was some kind of secret between them that she was not supposed to know about.

She decided to pretend she hadn't noticed anything

odd, and Staffa gradually relaxed. As usual, the gold tea-pot was bubbling beside Lady Matilda's chair. Staffa made her a huge cup of Haw-haw tea, and then another — and another, and another, until Jane stopped counting.

Lady Matilda was in a strange mood — excited and giggly. If she hadn't been drinking tea, Jane might have thought she was drunk.

"Oh, to BLAZES with the diet!" shouted Lady Matilda. "I'll have TEN of those weeny chocolate mousses — this is a NATIONAL EMERGENCY!"

When the chocolate mousses arrived (brought by a rather scared-looking waitress) Lady Matilda began to sing:

> Oh, hark to the tale of Tornado the spider,
> Who won the Queen's Cup
> With Batsindo, his rider!

Staffa rolled her eyes at Jane. "Take no notice. She always sings when she's had too much."

It was a very long song, and Jane could not make out all the verses — lots of burbled stuff about a jockey named Batsindo, who saw a bad omen in his breakfast on the day of the race. Lady Matilda was still singing when the three of them were going upstairs to bed. "This is the pad sart," she told them foggily, "I mean, the sad part." Suddenly tearful, she sang:

> When they reached the third plughole,
> Batsindo, he cried,
> Farewell, my dear mother!
> Farewell, my sweet bride!
> And he fell down the plughole,
> So hairy and wide!

"I'm so sorry you had to see this, Jane," Staffa said, unlocking the bedroom door while Lady Matilda — still singing — sagged against the wall. "She doesn't do it often. I think she's suffering from shock because her hat caught fire. Good night."

Jane lay awake in her strange hotel bed for ages. She missed her bedroom at home, with its faded Postman Pat wallpaper. She missed her own bed, with its comfy, twanging old mattress. And she had been alarmed by Lady Matilda's weird behavior — though she couldn't help laughing to herself, as she remembered her ladyship hooting out that meaningless song in her smoking hat.

When she finally fell asleep, Jane had an amazing

dream. She dreamed that Lady Matilda was standing in front of her, pulling up the skirt of her blue satin gown. Under the skirt, she wore a pair of huge frilly bloomers (in her dream, Jane made a huge effort not to giggle at the sight of these).

There seemed to be a secret pocket on the inside of the left leg. Lady Matilda took out something small and very bright that shot out light like little bolts of lightning. She loomed over Jane's bed. Her big, painted face came closer and closer, until Jane wanted to scream. The small object that she had taken out of her bloomers flashed in Jane's eyes.

Jane did scream then, and it woke her up. She had left the bedside lamp on, and it was comforting to see the tidy, boring hotel furniture. What a ridiculous dream, she thought. She drifted back to sleep, smiling to herself as she remembered the bloomers.

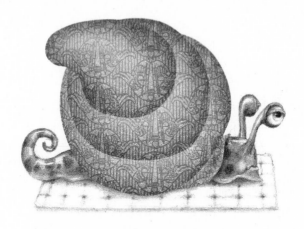

THE LIGHT

JANE WOKE THE NEXT MORNING WHEN STAFFA knocked at her door.

"Good morning, Jane. I hope you slept well. Mother says you're to wear the blue skirt with a yellow cardigan and tights."

"Can't I choose what I wear?" Jane asked crossly.

Staffa shook her head. "You'll find it easier just to do as she says."

"She's very bossy," Jane couldn't help saying.

"That, my dear Jane, is putting it mildly. She's used to being in charge, you see — everyone obeys her at home.

You'll look odd if you don't." Staffa glanced at her watch. "We're having breakfast in that private room. Don't be long, will you?"

Jane took a shower in her private bathroom (total bliss for a girl who normally shared a bathroom with six boys and a ton of mud), and dressed herself according to Lady Matilda's bossy instructions. The skirt and cardigan looked very nice when she put them on, and this made her less cross.

Staffa and her mother were already waiting in the private dining room. Lady Matilda was wearing a sort of soldier's jacket, with a matching peaked cap, in very bright shades of red and blue that made her look like a giant piece of Christmas chocolate.

"Jane, my dear child!" Lady Matilda said. "I'm afraid I've had some rather annoying news. I won't bore you with the details, but something has come up, and I will have to leave you and Staffa to travel alone for a couple of days."

"You're leaving us?" Jane tried not to sound hopeful.

"Yes, but Prockwald knows where he's going, and it's not for long."

Staffa looked worried. "Are you sure it's still all right to bring Jane?"

"Of course!" cried Lady Matilda. "Jane absolutely

MUST come home with us! But there are one or two little things that have to be settled first — and I'm the only person able to deal with them. So I'll meet you in a couple of days."

"May we buy some presents for the Boy Garden?"

"Oh, yes — what a sweet idea. Help yourself to money from the place in the car."

"Thanks, Mother!" Staffa grinned at Jane.

"Before I leave, however," Lady Matilda said, "I must remind you — both of you — to take very special care of the painted box." The box was resting on a chair beside her. She patted it fondly. "Remember that it must never be tilted or jolted, but carried upright at all times. Staffa, if you're walking any distance with the box, please wear the harness — we can't risk dropping it."

"Yes, Mother."

Jane saw that the painted box was immensely valuable. Staffa and her mother were very serious.

"When you arrive at the hotel tonight," Lady Matilda went on, "don't allow anyone else to carry the box to its room. And don't forget to set the two candlesticks in front of it right away. You'd better keep the key to the box's room under your pillow. Most important of all — Jane, I hope you're listening to this!"

"Yes, Lady Matilda."

"Most important of all, THE BOX MUST NEVER BE OPENED! Do you understand?"

"Yes!" Jane gasped. When Lady Matilda yelled like that, it was like being caught in a strong gust of wind.

"Oh dear, I don't like leaving it behind!"

Staffa said, "Don't worry, we'll take care of it."

"Well, I'll have to trust you. Don't forget that little bit of shopping either."

"No, Mother," Staffa said patiently. "You've reminded me a million times."

"Please don't be flippant, Staffa — these are vital winter supplies." Lady Matilda stood up, looming over the breakfast table in her gaudy uniform, like a shiny painted figure in a fairground. "Well, have a nice time, dears."

She swooped to kiss them both (Jane was unpleasantly reminded of her dream), and strode out of the room.

Staffa and Jane stared at each other, hardly able to believe the sudden silence.

"We're free," Staffa said. "We can do whatever we like!"

"We have to get that vital winter shopping," Jane said.

"The chocolate, you mean."

"Chocolate? I thought it must be medicine, or incubators for babies, or something."

"Where we come from, Jane, chocolate is a very valuable commodity — highly prized, and worth a lot of money."

"Is it?" Jane had never heard of anywhere like this. Staffa's home must be a very long way from the shops, she thought.

It was lovely to be alone with Staffa. Once Staffa had paid the bill (in cash), they set out in very high spirits. Prockwald drove them to a neat little market town, like King's Lumpton, but with smarter shops.

Staffa reached into the pouch for another thick pile of cash. "I'll leave Mother's list in the chocolate shop — then we can buy some presents for the boys. I want a red tricycle for little Ted, Gameboys for the twins — "

"Gameboys! You can't buy them expensive stuff like that!"

"Why not?"

Jane said, "I don't know. But it just doesn't seem right. You've given us so much already. I don't think my parents will like it."

Staffa surprised her by grabbing both her hands. "Please, Jane — please! Nobody ever lets me do anything! And it would make me so happy! I've never had any proper friends before!" Her little voice was shrill with pleading, and she looked very childish. "This money isn't any use to me. Just for once in my life, I'd like to spend it in a way that will bring happiness!"

"Oh, well," Jane said. Her parents might be a bit

uneasy about expensive presents, but she wasn't going to argue anymore — it meant a lot to Staffa, and the boys would be thrilled.

Staffa took her mother's list into a small shop called "The Fine Chocolate Company" and then she and Jane bought wonderful presents for everyone at the Boy Garden, including Leonard the horse. It was fantastic fun. Some of the shop assistants looked rather doubtful when Staffa paid with her pile of cash — a couple of them held the bills up to the light in a suspicious way — but she always told them she was "Spending my birthday money." And Jane noticed that she took care not to buy too much from the same shop.

"We'll wrap them tonight, at the hotel," Staffa said happily. "And then we'll get the hotel to post them tomorrow. Won't the boys be pleased when they open the parcels?"

Jane laughed. "Are you kidding? They'll go crazy!"

"I wish I could see little Ted's face," Staffa said wistfully.

"Staffa, there must be some way you can come back to the Boy Garden!" For the first time, Jane thought how dull it would be at home without her new best friend. "Can't you persuade Lady Matilda to let you visit us again?"

Staffa sighed and shook her head. "It's no use."

"But why?"

"You'll understand when you see my home. Now, let's have some lunch — something Mother doesn't like, since she's not here."

They had burgers, which neither of their mothers liked. When they returned to the car, they found Prockwald and a man in an apron loading dozens of boxes of fine chocolate into the trunk. Staffa paid the chocolate shop with more cash from the pouch in the seat — did the money in there ever run out? Jane's head was spinning with forbidden food and fizzy drinks, and the intoxicating pleasure of luxury shopping. Now that Lady Matilda was out of the way, she was having the time of her life.

Prockwald drove them to another country hotel. Once again, the painted box had its own room. Once again, Staffa set it very carefully on the table, flanked by its guard of gold candlesticks. When this was all done, she locked the door with an air of relief.

Jane asked, "Why does the box need a room to itself — I mean, wouldn't it be much cheaper if it shared your room? And why do you have to do the thing with the candlesticks?"

"Oh, you'll find out," Staffa said vaguely. "Sorry, but I can't explain it in any way you'd understand."

Jane saw that she'd have to be satisfied with this, as

Staffa was frowning and wearing her stubborn look. But she knew that Staffa and her mother had a secret, and she longed to know what it was. There had to be some explanation for the odd things that kept happening — the money pouch in the car, which never seemed to be empty; the way the two of them seemed to worship the painted box; the mysterious "business" that had taken Lady Matilda away. She decided not to ask Staffa so many questions, but to keep her eyes open.

As long as Jane didn't mention anything awkward, she and Staffa had a great evening in her hotel room. They phoned the Boy Garden — careful not to mention either the presents or the fact that Lady Matilda was not with them. They ordered room service for dinner, drank more fizzy drinks from the mini-bar and watched a movie on the television.

"Jane, this is utter paradise," sighed Staffa. "I wish we could spend the whole vacation like this."

"Don't you want to go home?"

"Only while you're there," Staffa said. "It's going to be ghastly when you have to leave — but let's not think about that now."

The next day, there was more driving. Jane asked where they were going, but Staffa only said it was "in the

North." They drove past villages, fields, woods and rivers. Very occasionally, the huge car drove along a stretch of highway. Mostly, however, Prockwald stuck to the smallest roads — empty lanes, winding tracks — full of signposts to towns Jane had never heard of. All she knew for certain was that they were now in Scotland. They stopped only briefly, to buy sandwiches for lunch and a tartan tin of shortbread for Lady Matilda.

"Mother likes to eat it for breakfast," Staffa said, "spread with snail paste."

"With what?"

Staffa looked embarrassed. "Sorry — chocolate paste. Slip of the tongue."

The scenery around them became wild and windswept. Jane saw bare hillsides and dark woods. As the light began to fade, she watched for the hotel where they would be staying. There was not a building in sight. They drove on and on, until they came to a flat, gray sea. Prockwald stopped the car at a deserted jetty, where a large, flat boat was waiting.

Jane saw that they had reached the very edge of Scotland. She asked, "Do we get out here?" She shivered. This place was bleak and blustery, and spookily empty, and felt like the edge of the whole world. Where was the wonderful castle she had been promised?

"No," Staffa said. "We stay in the car. The crossing doesn't take long."

"Where are we going?"

"To our island."

"You OWN an island? Seriously?" Jane hadn't known such a thing was possible.

"It's too late to get to my home, so we'll be spending the night with Mr. and Mrs. Prockwald, at their farmhouse."

Jane whispered, "Is Prockwald's wife like him? I mean, does she talk?"

"All the time," Staffa assured her. "And she's an excellent cook too."

Prockwald drove the car right onto the flat boat. It pulled slowly out into the sea. Jane looked out of the window, and saw nothing but gray sea all around them, as if the car were driving on water. In the gathering darkness, rocked by the waves, Jane and Staffa both fell asleep.

JANE WOKE SLOWLY, WITH A FEELING THAT SOMETHING wasn't right. They were driving again, on a bumpy road. There was some kind of light shining through her closed eyelids. Was it already morning?

She opened her eyes. Outside the window, everything was black. But the inside of the car was filled with an eerie silver light, extremely bright and as sharp as a blade.

It was pouring through a hairline crack in the painted box.

Jane was very scared. She wanted to wake Staffa, but she could not move or speak. The box was not on fire, because this light was too steady and too bright to come from flames, and there was no smoke. Could there be something electrical hidden inside the box, which they had switched on by mistake? She wished she knew more about science. Perhaps they were carrying something radioactive — she was sure she had heard about radioactive things glowing in the dark. Had Lady Matilda left them in charge of a nuclear bomb?

Calm down, she ordered herself. Nobody puts a nuclear bomb in a painted box — not even Lady Matilda was that crazy.

She hissed, "Staffa!"

And the eerie light was suddenly gone.

From the other side of the car, Staffa asked, "What is it?"

"Oh — I thought you were asleep — didn't you see it?"

"See what?"

"The light in the box — there was light inside the box — "

Staffa chuckled. "Jane, you're the one who's been asleep. You've been dreaming."

"It wasn't a dream, honestly. The light went out when I said your name."

"That's because you woke yourself up. You were dreaming."

"I was not!"

"There's no light in that box," Staffa said. "I wish I could open it, to show you."

"Why can't you open it? What's inside it?"

Staffa shrugged. "Family papers, I think. To tell the truth, I don't exactly know. But I can promise that you were dreaming when you saw that light of yours."

"Well — " Jane was still convinced that she had seen it, but began to wonder if her senses were playing tricks on her. She had to admit, it was a lot more likely to have been a dream. On the other hand, there was something very strange about this vacation, and it was getting stranger by the minute.

THE HOUSE AT THE
EDGE OF THE WORLD

THEY STOPPED VERY SUDDENLY, AT A HOUSE MA-rooned in a sea of darkness. Staffa carefully unfastened the box's seat belt, and gathered it in her arms.

Light spilled out of the open front door. Someone had come out to meet them. Jane could only guess it was a woman from her rounded shape — she was wearing builder's over-alls, and her face was wrapped in black scarves, like Prock-wald's. She helped both the girls out of the car, while her husband took their bags out of the trunk.

"Hello, Mrs. P.," Staffa said, giving the scarves an affectionate kiss, and handing over the box. "Any news from my mother?"

"Yes, Miss Staffa. The spot of bother is over, and everything's back to normal." Her voice was high and slow, like singing, with a happy lilt to it. "Welcome, Miss Jane. Please don't be put off by my black scarves. Me and my dear old husband are allergic to dust mites, and if we don't keep covered up, we sneeze our heads off. Now, the two of you had better come straight upstairs."

Jane felt less strange. The farmhouse was very bare and clean, but also warm and welcoming. Mrs. Prockwald's scarves weren't sinister once you knew about the dust mites, and there was something very sweet and reassuring about her voice. She certainly made up for her husband's silence.

"You'll find everything ready. I've put a simple supper of poached eggs and chocolate cake in each of your bedrooms. Lady Matilda says you must both go to bed at once, and not stay up talking till all hours."

Staffa yawned noisily. "Well, I don't mind. I'm extremely tired. Aren't you, Jane?"

"Er — yes," Jane said. "Yes, of course." She was far too curious to think of sleeping, and particularly curious to know where the box would be spending the night.

Mrs. Prockwald led them upstairs to a large landing with several doors. She opened one of these. Jane looked into a tiny room, little more than a cupboard, with nothing in it except a table.

Mrs. Prockwald put the box on the table, set out the gold candlesticks and briskly shut the door on it. "The room's a bit basic, but the box won't mind roughing it for one night. There isn't a key, but you won't need one here — it couldn't be safer."

While she talked, Mrs. Prockwald led Jane into a large, warm bedroom. It didn't have much furniture, but there were cheerful lamps and curtains, and a real fire. On a small table in front of the fire was a peculiar supper of two poached eggs, a large chocolate cake and nothing else.

"The bathroom's between your two bedrooms, Miss Jane — you'll be sharing it with Miss Staffa."

"Thank you, Mrs. P.," Staffa said, yawning again. "We'd better get some sleep. Good night, Jane."

She went into her own room and shut the door. Mrs. Prockwald went downstairs. Left alone, Jane sat on her bed, listening. She sat very still, until the house was silent, and all she could hear was the drumming of her own heart. She had made a decision. She was going to break her promise to Lady Matilda — she couldn't stand not knowing anymore.

Shivering with excitement and fear, she took off her

shoes, and crept out of her bedroom as quietly as she could. The landing was deserted. Slowly and very carefully, Jane opened the door of the box's room and slipped inside.

The tiny room was dark, but there was just enough moonlight coming through the window to see by. Jane's mouth was dry. If Lady Matilda ever found out about this, what would she do?

Very, very cautiously, she opened the lid of the painted box about half an inch. There was light inside it, but of a different quality than the light she had seen in the car. Jane crouched down, put her eye against the opening — and gasped aloud.

She was looking into a miniature room, like a room in a doll's house. But the room inside the box was more detailed than any doll's house she had ever seen. Every tiny thing in it was perfect. There were little sofas and tables, bookcases filled with tiny books and tiny paintings on the walls. A tiny fire glowed in the grate. Jane thought it was adorable. She let out her breath in a great sigh of relief. They had not been carrying a nuclear bomb, or anything like it. Lady Matilda had been making all this song and dance about a beautiful toy.

And then something terrible happened.

In the tiny room, the door opened. A tiny figure with dark hair walked into the room. It stretched and yawned, and stirred the fire with a tiny poker. It picked up a tiny book from a tiny round table beside one of the sofas.

It was Staffa.

Jane felt giddy and slightly sick. This had to be a dream, or a hallucination. Or some kind of trick. This could not be real.

She watched, fascinated and horrified, as the tiny Staffa tucked the book under her arm and walked around the tiny room, switching off all the lamps. When she had finished she walked out, closing the tiny door behind her. The inside of the painted box was now in darkness, except for the tiny orange glow of the fire.

Jane closed the box and left the room. Her fingers were trembling and clumsy, and she was covered in goose pimples when she heard the smallest sounds. She was very frightened, but she had to talk to Staffa — this time, Staffa would have to give her a proper explanation.

She tried the door of Staffa's room. It was locked. She went into their shared bathroom — and the door leading to Staffa's room was also locked.

Her bed's empty, Jane thought; she's inside the box, and I'm alone here.

She sat down on her bed to think things over.

First, there had been the dream about Lady Matilda, then the light in the box, and now this. Staffa had said she was seeing things. Either she was going crazy, or the secret of the box was very strange indeed.

Her room was bright and cheerful, and Jane became calmer. She suddenly remembered she was hungry, and ate the poached eggs and a small slice of chocolate cake. It was after midnight and she was very tired — but she couldn't sleep. She was itching to take another look at the box.

Once again, she crept across the landing. She crept into the box's room. Taking a deep breath, she lifted the lid of the box about four inches — and saw nothing but the inside of an empty wooden box.

The relief nearly made her laugh out loud. There was no tiny room. It had been another of those waking dreams she'd been having lately — probably, she decided, because she was tired. She went back to her room and went to bed.

THE FIRST THING JANE HEARD WHEN SHE WOKE UP WAS the sound of singing. She opened her eyes. The room was filled with morning sunlight, so fresh and bright that she longed to be outside. Mrs. Prockwald was setting plates out on the round table, singing a song with words that Jane couldn't quite make out — something like, "his heart was as big as a beetle's leg." She sat up.

"Good morning, Miss Jane!" sang Mrs. Prockwald. "I've brought you a slice of ham and a fruitcake. Lady Matilda says to eat it all up, because you've got a long walk this morning."

"Lady Matilda? Is she here?" Jane couldn't help sounding disappointed — they had been having so much fun without her.

"Yes, dear, she's downstairs. She says to wear your boy's trousers and shoes."

Jane took her Boy Garden clothes out of her backpack and put them on. After the girly things Lady Matilda had bought her, they felt like comfortable old friends. She was hungry, but she couldn't face the fruitcake or the slice of ham — Mrs. Prockwald had some funny ideas about food.

STAFFA WAS WAITING IN THE HALL DOWNSTAIRS. "WELL, Jane, are you ready?"

Jane asked, "Ready for what?"

"Today is the day. We're taking you home. You'll sleep tonight in our castle."

"Your castle must be a very long way away," Jane said. "I looked out of my window and there doesn't seem to be a single building for miles around — nothing but bare hills."

Staffa said, "You'll see. It's quite a hike, I'm afraid."

"Ah, dear child!" Lady Matilda swept into the hall. She was dressed in an elaborate hiking costume of scarlet corduroy, and carrying a small pickax that looked like solid silver. "Our long journey is ending at last! Staffa, have you packed our lunch, dear?"

"Yes, Mother."

"Then let us set out to meet our destiny!"

Lady Matilda wore a sort of leather harness over her hiking clothes. Mrs. Prockwald carefully strapped the painted box into this harness, so that it rode underneath her ladyship's great bosom like a baby in a sling. Staffa took the bag with the gold candlesticks. Jane wondered what was happening to the rest of their luggage, but didn't like to ask. The three of them walked out into the bright morning. Jane turned back, to see Mr. and Mrs. Prockwald at the front door of their lonely house, bowing very low.

They began to climb a steep and stony hillside.

"This may be a hard walk for you, my dear Jane," Lady Matilda said. "We'll do our best not to tire you out."

She threw back her shoulders and began to sing:

I love to go a-wandering,

Back to my mountain home!

Fol-de-ri! Fol-de-ra — Ugh! Ugh! — oh,

I need to sit down!

Lady Matilda was a very slow walker. She huffed and groaned, and her face turned as scarlet as her suit. Jane, who found the climb easy, couldn't believe what a wimp she was.

They climbed for the rest of the morning. Jane rather enjoyed it. There was a cool breeze that smelled of the sea, and it felt wonderfully refreshing after all those days in the car.

"Here we are!" gasped Lady Matilda. "Home at last!"

Jane looked around, very puzzled. They stood on a bald hillside, a few feet from a heap of boulders. Scrubby grass and rocks surrounded them as far as the eye could see. Where was the famous castle?

Lady Matilda collapsed on a tuft of grass. "Oof! I can't move another inch! Jane, dear, do you see that heap of big stones?"

"Yes," Jane said. Of course she saw it. There was nothing else for miles.

"Do you see those two biggest stones, right at the bottom?"

"Yes."

"Take the box and put it between those two stones, as far back as it will go. Do you understand?"

"Yes," Jane said again. Lady Matilda's voice had become hard and strict and more than a little scary, and there was no question of disobeying.

Lady Matilda unbuckled the leather harness. Jane took the box, and carried it to the boulders. She found the two big stones at the bottom of the heap. The box slotted neatly between them.

"Now stand very still," Staffa said. "Stay exactly where you are, and don't move."

Her sharp face pale and determined, she began to walk slowly towards Jane. As she walked, she pulled at the gold ring she wore on her right hand.

"Staffa? What're you doing?"

"Keep still!"

"Wait a minute," said Lady Matilda, settling her scarlet cape. "Don't forget our lunch."

Staffa sighed impatiently. "Don't you ever think about anything else?"

"You'll think about it too, young lady, when you're hungry and there's nothing to eat."

"Oh, all right. Sorry about this, Jane." Staffa took

from her pocket one chocolate truffle. She put this carefully on the ground, close to the toe of Jane's sneaker.

"Look, what's going on?" Jane demanded. "Where's
your house?"

Staffa said, "There are one or two little things I forgot
to tell you about our home. To be honest, I was afraid that
you'd refuse to come if you knew."

"Knew what? Staffa, what are you talking about?"

Staffa took Jane's right hand. "It's best to keep as still
as you can. It might hurt a little, but don't be scared — it
doesn't last long." She pushed her gold ring onto Jane's
little finger.

Jane screamed. The cold band of metal became tighter
and tighter, until the pain was agonizing. Just when her
bone was on the point of snapping, the pain suddenly
stopped. Something like a huge gust of wind knocked her
violently off her feet. Everything was dark around her.
She was

Falling,

Falling,

Falling,

— and then nothing.

A TRUFFLE AS BIG AS THE RITZ

WHEN HER STUNNED SENSES RECOVERED, SHE FOUND that she was lying on the ground, in the depths of a forest. The trees were strange, she thought fuzzily — great reedy green trunks, with not a leaf between them. She blinked hard several times, trying to clear her blurred eyes. She could see Lady Matilda a short distance away, sitting with her back against one of the strange trees. She took a mirror and a lipstick from her handbag, and began to repaint her big red lips. Jane could not move or speak. It felt like watching someone in a dream.

There was a clanking sound. Through the trees came

the most disgusting creature Jane had ever seen — black and metallic, and the size of a carthorse, with huge eyes like colanders and long, hairy legs. This thing shuffled towards Matilda. Jane tried to scream.

Lady Matilda glanced up at the horrible creature, and tutted crossly "Staffa! Staffa! Where are you? You know I hate ants!"

In her crazy dream, Jane saw Staffa, carrying a rifle. Very calmly, she shot the creature in the head. It fell slowly to the ground like collapsing scaffolding.

"Calm down, Mother," Staffa said. "No such thing as a picnic without ants."

"Yuck, dreadful things! And don't they smell nasty when they're dying? It's enough to put you off your food. Is Jane awake yet?"

Jane tried to say that she was awake. The words would not come out.

"No," she heard Staffa say. "But she seems fine. We might get her through it without too severe a shock — as long as you don't frighten her."

"Oh, pooh," Lady Matilda said gaily. "She's one of us now, and she might as well get used to it."

Suddenly, Jane knew what had happened. She had once looked at an ant through a magnifying glass, and it had been exactly like this dead black monster. And if the monster was an ant, these strange trees might be blades of grass — that far-off mountain the heap of boulders. The three of them had shrunk until they were smaller than insects. They were even smaller than the tiny Staffa she had seen (or dreamed of seeing) inside the box. This nightmare was mind-boggling. Why couldn't she wake up?

"No, dear Jane, you're not dreaming," Lady Matilda said, smiling. "This is perfectly real. You have entered the Kingdom of Eck. I think you may continue to call Princess Staffa by her first name — but you must address me as 'Your Majesty.'"

Jane was beyond surprise. She sat up in a daze, listening to the trumpeting tones of the woman who said she was a queen.

"To cut a long story short, my dear Jane, we are taking you back to our palace. There you will meet our son, King Quarles the Seventh — Staffa's big brother."

Jane turned to Staffa. "Your brother's a king?" (King of what?)

"Now you can see why I couldn't tell you the truth," Staffa said. "You'd never have believed me — and I did so want to bring you home with me! I wanted it so much! If you hate it, you can go straight home! Do you hate it?"

"I — I don't know," Jane said, still fuzzy. "Are you sure this isn't a dream?"

"Positive. This is as real as the Boy Garden. I can't wait to show it to you."

"But first," Queen Matilda said, "we will have lunch." She stood up, huffing and puffing, brushing specks of soil from her scarlet knickerbockers.

Jane noticed a large round hump of gleaming dark brown, about the size of a garden shed. The queen walked over to it. She swung her silver pickax into its smooth surface, until it cracked loudly.

"You do the rest, Staffa — a nice big piece for me, please." Queen Matilda took a large white napkin from her handbag and tucked it under her chin.

Staffa had a long knife. She went up to the brown hump, and hacked out a jagged piece the size of a paving stone. Queen Matilda snatched it, and her great red lips began to chomp at it greedily. There was a powerful smell of chocolate. Jane realised that the brown hump was the chocolate truffle Staffa had placed on the ground. She was hungry, but the heavy clod of chocolate Staffa gave her made her feel sick. She could only take one bite.

The queen ate two large slices, with grunts of pleasure. "Oh, this is sublime! You will learn, dear Jane, that there is a tragic shortage of sugar in our kingdom. Waste not, want not — I'll tell the Gull Patrol to bring the rest of the truffle home for tea."

Staffa said, "They won't be able to spare the officers."

The queen was irritated. "Nonsense, officers can always be spared. Now, let us begin our journey. I told Quarley we'd be back in time for dinner."

Jane dared to ask, "Where are we going?"

"The box, of course," Staffa said. "On the other side of this forest."

"Forest? Oh, you mean the grass."

"Yes." Staffa picked up her rifle. "I'll go first. You stick close to Mother."

"What's the Gull Patrol?"

Staffa was grim. "I hope you never have to find out."

The three of them walked through the huge stalks of grass in single file. Staffa went first, then Jane, then the queen. The light was gloomy, and there was a strong smell of cut lawn. After about half an hour, Staffa shot another ant.

This was all so strange and so fascinating that Jane had stopped being frightened. The world was very different when you were tiny. The grass was alive with insects, some so small that she would never have been able to see them with a normal human eye. They passed a large black beetle, as tall as Queen Matilda, with a big back like shiny plastic and busy claws like pliers. Jane was nervous, but Staffa assured her that it was harmless. It bumbled about clumsily, sniffing at the ground, and took no notice of the three miniature humans.

A seagull cried above them.

Staffa shouted, "It's seen us! Get down!"

Queen Matilda — without a thought for her posh clothes — screamed and flung herself to the ground. A black shadow fell across them.

"Jane — get down!" Staffa yelled.

The seagull swooped down towards them. It was an astonishing and fearful sight, like a jumbo jet landing in your backyard. Its huge beak opened. Jane dropped to the ground. Staffa bravely remained standing. She shot the great bird in its neck and its vast white belly. The bullet holes were tiny, but the seagull, with another deafening shriek, flew away.

"Well done, Staffa," panted Queen Matilda. "That was a close one! Help me up, girls."

Jane and Staffa helped the portly queen to her feet.

"On this side of the castle door," Staffa told Jane, "the gulls are our biggest menace. They swoop down on our people and carry them off in their beaks — we lost a whole platoon last week."

"The other birds mostly leave us alone," Queen Matilda said. "We've had a bit of bother with puffins, but they're not as clever as the gulls. Those horrid birds have developed a taste for us."

They walked on. Jane was careful to stick close to Staffa. She didn't fancy being carried off to some fishy-smelling nest — this new world was dangerous. She wondered when Staffa had learned to use a gun, and wished her brothers could have seen her firing it. Her stomach rumbled. She hoped there was some real food where they were going.

It was a long hike, but eventually, as the sun was sinking, they came out of the grass forest and saw the box.

"Home sweet home!" the queen said happily.

Jane had assumed that the paintings on the box would look coarse and false when she was tiny — but they were more exquisitely detailed than ever. She could swear there was a real sunset over the painted woods and hills, and she could almost see the painted branches stirring in a ghostly breeze. The air was full of strange scents, as if they had wafted out of the painted meadows.

The queen said, "Jane dear, run up to the box. Give it

three sharp knocks with the gold ring on your finger, then run back as fast as you can."

Jane walked up to the box, thinking that her hand would surely go straight through it. But the painted sides were hard. She knocked three times, with the ring Staffa had put on her finger.

"Back!" called Staffa. "Get back!"

Jane ran back to Staffa. Beneath her feet she felt the ground trembling. There was a loud rumbling sound, as if a giant machine had been switched on underneath the earth. She clutched Staffa's hand. The box shook alarmingly. Jane braced herself for an explosion. Instead, the sides of the box suddenly sprang apart.

Out of the box a castle unfolded, turret by turret. There was a shower of dust, and large pieces of stone crashed to the ground. Out of the castle towers, a beautiful landscape unfolded, covered with rich fields and woods. A great wind rose up, and the two landscapes — the bare Scottish island and the paintings on the box — whirled around them until the colors were a blur.

THE ECKERS

THE WIND DIED AS SUDDENLY AS IT HAD STARTED. Jane found that they were no longer tiny figures on a bald hillside, but three full-size people standing in front of a stone gateway. There was a real portcullis, a moat and a drawbridge, just like Mike and Phil's gray plastic castle at home. Brightly colored flags danced in the summer breeze.

"A real castle," Jane said. "Just like a fairytale." It was beautiful.

"Welcome to our palace, dear Jane," said Queen Matilda. "I hope you will come to consider it your second home."

They crossed the drawbridge. Two soldiers, wearing

uniforms of purple and orange, guarded the castle's entrance. Jane tried not to stare at them (not wanting to hurt their feelings) but she thought the soldiers looked very odd indeed. When you got close, you saw that they were not quite human. Their bodies were small and round, with long, skinny legs and arms. They had large heads of a peculiar triangular shape. Their eyes and mouths were also shaped like triangles. Their necks were very long and very thin, and they did not have chins. They bowed very low as the queen swept past them.

"Your Majesty!" Another triangular soldier came running out to meet them. Jane thought he must be more important than the others — his purple uniform was covered with rich gold embroidery. "Your Imperial Greatness! We didn't expect you so soon!"

He bowed, and kissed the queen's hand.

"Jane," said the queen, "this is Captain Hooter, my chief servant. Hooter, this is Miss Jane."

To Jane's embarrassment, Captain Hooter grabbed her hand and kissed it. "I'm honored, madam."

Nobody had ever called her "madam" — except Dad when he was being sarcastic. Her jeans and sweatshirt were stained with grass, soil and chocolate. She felt very small and dirty.

There were now dozens of triangular people milling

around them, their chinless heads bobbing on their elongated necks.

"Our servants," Staffa said.

"Is this what the Prockwalds look like under all those scarves?"

"Well, yes. They're not really allergic to dust mites. In your world, they have to cover themselves up."

Jane's world felt very far away. She gazed around the hall of the royal palace. It was magnificent — partly like a stately home and partly like a cathedral. Though it was summer, there was a fire in the enormous fireplace, as big as a burning house. There was a thick purple carpet and chairs heaped with soft velvet cushions. The walls were covered with pictures — portraits of kings and queens, and various triangular people, mostly in uniform. Above the fireplace was a huge painting of a hairy spider, with the word "Tornado" carved into the gold frame — the queen's beloved racing spider. Now that she was tiny, the thought of meeting a creature like the late Tornado made Jane shiver. She stayed close to Staffa.

The queen handed her silver pickax to Captain Hooter. "We left a chocolate truffle near the border. Tell the general to fetch it before dinner. And tell the cook to melt it for gravy."

"Yes, Your Majesty."

"Then go and find the king, and tell him I think he's very naughty not to come and meet me."

"Yes, Your Majesty."

Staffa gave Jane's hand a reassuring squeeze. "Don't worry, you'll soon get used to everything. This is Twilly, who will be your personal servant while you're staying here."

Twilly had a pink-and-white, triangular face and hair in fat curls like brown bedsprings. She looked about the same age as Jane and Staffa. She curtseyed. "How do you do, madam."

"But I don't need a servant," Jane protested. "I wouldn't know what to do with her!" She wanted to say that Twilly gave her the creeps.

"Oh, that's another thing you'll soon get used to," Staffa said breezily. "Twilly will run your baths and brush your hair and take care of your clothes. That's her job."

Jane took another look at Twilly. The funny little pot-bellied, spindly-legged creature gave her a beaming smile. She wore a black dress, with a long, full skirt, and a white apron thick with frills. Now that she was looking properly, Jane saw that there was something very sweet about Twilly's face. She smiled back, feeling a little less freaked out.

"Jane, my dear child," said the queen, "go to your room. Your maid will dress you for dinner — just the family, on your first evening. I must bustle off now, to sentence a couple of people to death." She flounced away through a stone arch, followed by Captain Hooter and a crowd of servants.

Jane shuddered. Had she really heard that? Since her shrinking, she had begun to notice a glint in Queen Matilda's eye that was decidedly nasty. She could well believe she sentenced people to death.

"Come on." Staffa tugged Jane's hand.

They followed Twilly up a massive marble staircase and along endless corridors full of paintings and large gold ornaments. Servants bowed and curtseyed as they passed.

Jane whispered, "I wish they wouldn't do that!"

"I told you, you'll get used to it." Staffa threw open a door. "This is your room."

"WOW!" Jane gasped. It was a bedroom from a fairytale. The latticed windows had elaborate curtains of pink silk. There was a white four-poster bed, a huge wardrobe and a bath in the shape of a flower. The taps were made of gold. "Is this really mine? Seriously?"

"Do you like it?"

Jane flopped down on the bed, sinking into the silk pillows. "It's incredible! I love it!"

"I'm so glad," Staffa said. "It's very important to me that you enjoy yourself here — I still feel bad because I didn't warn you. Unfortunately, there is no easy way to tell someone they'll be passing into another dimension. I hope you'll forgive me."

The light of the setting sun poured through the window. It fell on Staffa's bare arm, and Jane noticed how hard and how white her skin was.

She heard herself blurting out, "You're not human, are you?"

Staffa coolly raised her eyebrows. "Not really."

Jane was more curious than scared. "What are you, then?"

"It's complicated," Staffa said. "My family — the royal family of Eckwald — comes from a race of elves. But we have to marry full humans — like you. Or our race will die out."

"Was your father a full human?"

"Yes."

"Do any humans live here?"

Staffa smiled sourly. "Obviously not — you've seen how hard it is to bring a human through the box."

"But it's not hard for you," Jane said. "Your mother came back, didn't she? That night when her hat was on fire."

"Yes, well done. Mother and I can slip in and out

whenever we please, but humans can only pass through the one crossing point. And it has to be on our own remote island."

"Why?"

"So the box won't get stolen when we're not there to guard it — or kicked over by a sheep. It has to stay in a very safe place."

"What about . . . you know . . ." Jane nodded towards Twilly. "Is she partly human too?"

"Oh, she's just an Ecker," Staffa said. "The Eckers are quite different — another race entirely, mostly goblin with a dash of field mouse. They're not as clever as we are. That's why we have a stern duty to keep the royal family going. They need us."

Jane looked at Twilly to see if she minded this rude description of her people. But Twilly was busy dusting the glass bottles on the dressing table and didn't seem to have heard.

"Where is this place, Staffa?" she asked. "Is it part of my world?"

"Not really."

"Where did the huge spiders come from, then?"

Staffa said, "They were mostly brought in through the box by mistake, and the Eckers learned to farm them. Otherwise, we are completely outside your time and space."

This was not a comfortable idea. The Boy Garden seemed very, very far away.

Jane asked, "Who's being sentenced to death?"

"Ah, you heard." Staffa was embarrassed. "Just a few troublemakers — it's not as bad as it sounds."

"But that's terrible!"

"Take my advice," Staffa said, very seriously. "Try not to notice — and don't ask too many questions. Now I must dress for dinner." She hurried out of the room.

Jane swallowed several times, trying not to cry. This place was weird and dangerous. She was suddenly very homesick. Her watch said it was half past six. She pictured the messy kitchen at the Boy Garden. Mom would be taking little Ted upstairs for his bath. Dan and Jon would be playing loud music in their bedroom. Dad would be making the big pasta-and-tuna bake they always had on Wednesdays. She wished with all her heart that she could call them. Two hot tears spilled down her cheeks.

"Oh, madam!" Twilly cried. "Don't cry, my poor dear!" She sat down on the bed beside Jane and pushed a lace handkerchief into her hand. "Everything will be lovely — you'll see!"

Her curls bobbed around her head, and her eyes were full of kindness. She patted Jane with her warm little hand — Jane noticed that it had the smallness and delicacy of a mouse's paw, and that Twilly's ears were large and soft, a bit like the soft ears of a mouse. She remembered that Twilly's people — the Eckers — were partly descended from field mice. This must be why Twilly's pale blue eyes were so big and round.

"Tell you what, madam," said Twilly, "I'll fetch you a nice glass of buttercup juice."

Jane sniffed. "You don't have to do things for me."

Twilly giggled. "Oh, yes I do. I'm your private servant, and you've got to give me orders."

"But I don't know how to give orders!"

"Just think of the queen," Twilly said. "She never does anything else."

This made Jane giggle too, and she immediately felt better. "Okay, here's an order for you — stop calling me 'madam.' Just call me 'Jane.'"

Twilly's eyes widened. "I can't do that!"

"Why not?"

"If anyone heard me, I'd lose my job — and I don't want to go back to the palace laundry, madam. That's where I was working before, and there are no prospects for a bright girl like me."

"Well — " Jane already knew that she did not want to lose her kind little maid. "What about if you just call me 'Jane' in private?"

Twilly considered this. "All right — as long as nobody hears. Now, madam — Jane — let's choose a dress for dinner." She jumped off the bed and flung open the doors of the big wardrobe. "My cousin is the chief seamstress here, and she says these are the most wonderful gowns she ever made!"

For the umpteenth time that day, Jane could only gasp. This was fantasy run wild. The wardrobe was filled with fabulous dresses, in colors as pure and as vivid as the colors of the painted box.

"Which shall it be, madam — whoops! — I mean Jane? What about this dark yellow? It would look ever so nice with your lovely hair."

She took out a long dress, with a huge puffy skirt that swept the floor, and helped Jane to put it on. It fit perfectly, and felt as light and soft as a butterfly's wing.

Twilly twirled around her, clapping her hands. "Oh, how princessy you look! Sit down at the dressing table, and I'll do your hair."

Jane couldn't help being excited. When she sat down in front of the big dressing table mirror, she saw that she really did look as elegant as a real princess. This was especially thrilling for a girl who had always worn her brother's hand-me-downs. Wouldn't Ellie and Angie die of jealousy if they could see her now?

Twilly brushed her long red hair and pinned it up. As she worked busily, with her triangular mouth full of hairpins, she sang to herself. The words were mumbled, but Jane heard "beetle's leg" and realized this was the song sung by Mrs. Prockwald.

"Twilly, what are you singing?"

"Don't you know it? Of course you don't. But you'll hear it a lot — the whole city's singing it at the moment. It's Migorn's latest."

"Who?"

"Migorn, that's who." Twilly was eager. "The best singer in the whole world! I hope you get to see her at the theater."

There was a knock at the door. Twilly opened it, with a deep curtsey.

It was Staffa, dressed in something long and stiff in pale blue. "Jane — you look absolutely lovely! Now let's get down to dinner. We mustn't keep her waiting."

They walked through what seemed like miles and miles of corridors, until they reached a large dining room.

"At last!" cried the braying voice of the queen. "I'm starving!"

Queen Matilda was at the top of the long table, in a big chair like a throne. She wore a scarlet dress of thick velvet and a glittering crown. Beside her, on a smaller throne, sat a handsome young man with dark hair — Staffa's brother, Jane guessed. He looked about the same age as Jane's brother Martin. He wore a plain black uniform and a plain gold crown.

Staffa whispered in Jane's ear, "Curtsey!"

Jane dropped a deep curtsey. It didn't feel silly in this long dress.

"Well, Quarley, here she is," said the queen. "This is the souvenir we brought back from our travels. Doesn't she look perfect? Jane, this is my son, His Majesty, King Quarles."

Jane decided to curtsey again.

"Hello, Jane," the young king said. "Welcome to my country. I hope you'll have a very pleasant visit."

"Thank you, Your Majesty."

"Oh, don't bother with all that nonsense," the king said. "Call me Quarley."

Captain Hooter directed Jane to the chair next to Quarley. Staffa sat opposite. Jane soon stopped feeling shy. The queen was busy eating, and took no more notice of her. The young king was very friendly, and he asked lots of questions about her home. It was like talking to Martin or Dan. Jane's mom would have said he was a "nice boy." When he was not smiling, however, Quarley's pale face was very sad. Jane wondered why.

He helpfully explained the strange food. "You might not want the steak — it's carved off a slug."

"You're joking!"

Staffa and Quarley chuckled at Jane's horror.

"I'm afraid not," said Quarley. "We keep herds of slugs here. You should see the great beasts glistening in the rising sun!"

Jane shuddered. She had always detested slugs, and the idea of meeting an enormous one — let alone a herd of them — was revolting.

Staffa said, "They're a bit like cows in your world. They taste great."

"No way! What's the green stuff?"

"Mashed stalk of celandine," Quarley said. "In a sauce of wild honey and snail's milk. The brown stuff is a kind of soft honey cake, and the round white thing is snail's cheese."

Jane was extremely hungry. She couldn't remember the last time she had eaten proper food. This food (particularly the slug steak) sounded disgusting, yet the smells wafting up from her plate were oddly tempting. She dared to take a forkful of the green mush. It was rather good — a bit like mashed potatoes, with hints of broccoli, yogurt and daffodil. She ate it quickly, and tried the soft brown cake. It was deliciously light and sweet. Before she really knew what she was doing, Jane had taken a bite of the steak. This was also delicious.

The dessert, carried in by Captain Hooter on a huge silver tray, was lumps of the chocolate truffle swimming in a hot chocolate sauce.

"Yum!" cried the queen. She shoveled it in with a large spoon like a trowel. "Aren't you having some, Quarley?"

"No thank you, Mother. The girls can have my share."

Afterwards, when Jane and Staffa were walking back to their bedrooms, Staffa said, "Quarley's nice, isn't he?"

"Very nice. But why is he so sad?"

For a second, Staffa looked a little wary. Then she shrugged, deliberately vague. "Oh, it's lonely being one of us."

"Has Quarley ever had a human friend?"

"Good grief, Jane," Staffa said. "It's nearly midnight — don't you ever get tired of asking questions?"

"But has he? I mean, has he ever been to my world?"

"Yes," Staffa said shortly. "Here we are, at your door. Good night Jane. Sleep well."

She almost ran away down the long corridor, leaving

Jane to wonder what on earth she was hiding. What was wrong with asking questions?

In Jane's bedroom, Twilly was waiting with a cup of hot snail milk and honey. She unfastened Jane's dress and helped her into a soft white nightgown. She brushed her hair and helped her into the great, soft, silken bed. Now that she had a full stomach, Jane was incredibly tired. This bed was blissful. It was like lying in a warm cloud. She stopped fretting about her unanswered questions and fell asleep.

THE OLD PRINCESS

WHEN JANE OPENED HER EYES THE NEXT MORNING, the first thing she saw was the beaming face of Twilly.

"Good morning, Your Janeship."

Jane sat up. "What did you call me?"

"I was a bit worried about calling you just 'Jane,'" Twilly said seriously. "So I've decided to call you, 'Your Janeship.' That way I won't get into too much trouble if anyone hears me."

"Okay, I don't want to get you into trouble." Jane was too sleepy to argue. "Is it raining outside?"

"No indeed, Your Janeship, it's a lovely sunny day."

"But I can hear thunder — there it is again!"

"That's not thunder," Twilly said. "That's just the guns."

"Guns?" Jane was properly awake now. "Where?"

"Just outside the palace walls, Your Janeship."

"What are they firing at?"

"Us in the palace, of course!" Twilly said cheerfully.

"*What?*"

There was a mighty explosion, so close that the ornaments on the mantlepiece rattled. A thin shower of plaster dust fell from the ceiling.

Twilly said, "T-t-t!" and whisked the dust away with her little feather duster. She did not seem at all bothered by the gunfire.

"Twilly, who's firing at us?"

"Nothing to worry about, your Janeship." Twilly held out a pink dressing gown. "I expect there's been another revolution. Your bath's all ready for you."

"What do you mean?" Jane was scared. She had seen revolutions on the news — they were always full of shouting and shooting, and terrible fighting. "When did it happen?"

Twilly refused to say anymore. She simply pursed up her triangular mouth and shook her bouncing bedspring curls. She had laid out a green silk dress, with a long skirt and tight sleeves.

Jane looked at it gloomily. "Why can't I wear the things I came in?"

"Sorry, Your Janeship. The queen told me to burn them. I put them in the boiler."

"She's such a cow," Jane said crossly. "I'd like to burn some of her stupid clothes."

Outside the window, voices shouted angrily. There was another explosion, followed by the sound of breaking glass.

Jane screamed and clung to Twilly. "Please — tell me what's going on!"

Twilly was afraid. She lowered her voice to a whisper. "You mustn't notice it — you mustn't say anything! If you mention it, the queen goes crazy! One of my sisters was a serving girl here, and she got sacked because a bullet came through the window and shot the dessert right out of her hands, and she screamed."

"Are you telling me you're more scared of the queen than you are of the guns?"

"Oh yes," Twilly said feelingly. "She's a terror. She had my poor sister whipped."

"But that's awful! Your sister didn't do anything wrong!"

"She mentioned the unmentionable," Twilly said. "Nobody does that here."

Jane soon found that this was only too true. Captain Hooter escorted her to the royal breakfast parlor, and she found the royal family sitting around a small table, apparently without a care in the world. The guns thundered and boomed outside, and they carried on eating their breakfast. King Quarles was reading a kind of newspaper (very thin and crackly, with no pictures). Queen Matilda was eating more of the chocolate truffle. Both were wearing army uniforms.

Bullets cracked and whistled outside. An angry voice yelled, "Death to the oppressors!"

"Good morning, Jane," the queen said. "Did you sleep well?"

"Yes, Your Majesty." Remembering Twilly's warning, Jane made a great effort not to look scared. She even managed to eat a couple of bites of fried slug.

"I was just wondering what we should do today," piped Staffa, "but I'm afraid we can't go out. We'll have to resort to rainy-day amusements."

The window suddenly smashed, showering the nearby servants with broken glass. A large bomb — black and fizzing, like a bomb in a cartoon — landed in the middle of the breakfast table.

Queen Matilda sighed impatiently. "This is ridiculous! Quarley, put it in the sand bucket. And tell Hooter to arrest all the usual people."

King Quarles (still looking at the newspaper and chewing his breakfast) calmly picked up the bomb and dropped it into a large tub of sand under the table.

"I'm glad to see that you're being sensible about this, Jane," said the queen. "I should explain that certain Eckers are always plotting against the royal family. They have a silly idea that they should be ruling themselves, instead of leaving us to do it for them."

Quarley folded his newspaper. His face was very pale and sad, but he gave the girls an encouraging smile. "You mustn't mind if you're left alone for a few days, just until we can sort this out." He added, "It might be a good idea to keep away from the windows."

THE REST OF THAT DAY, AND THE DAYS AFTER, WERE A mixture of fear and incredible, groaning boredom. Jane and Staffa were only allowed to go into each other's bedrooms and the palace library. The queen and Quarley were busy putting down the latest revolution — the queen was commander-in-chief of the army, and Quarley was fighting with the Students' Corps from his university.

The two girls were expected to keep well out of the way.

There was nothing to do — no television to watch, no radio, no CDs. The library (the room Jane had seen when she opened the box) had nothing but very dull books by generals and politicians. She would have gone crazy, if it hadn't been for Twilly.

The kind little servant girl was the first person Jane saw each morning. She was cheerful and funny, and full of fascinating stories about life among the Eckers. As the dull days passed, Twilly spent more and more time with Jane, until she had turned into a real friend.

Jane couldn't help noticing, however, that this new friendship annoyed Staffa.

"You're supposed to be MY friend!" Staffa complained. "But whenever I want to talk to you, you're always with that Ecker!"

"Well, why don't you join us?" Jane asked. "She's really fun, Staffa — she knows all Migorn's songs, and some of her stories would make you die laughing."

"Don't be silly. I can't possibly join you."

"Why not?"

"She's an Ecker."

Jane was tired of this argument. "Well, what if she is? What's wrong with being an Ecker?"

"They're not like us," Staffa said coldly.

"Have you ever spoken to an Ecker?" Jane demanded.

"Of course, don't be silly. I've been surrounded by Eckers all my life!"

"Yes, but they're your servants. I meant, have you ever had a proper talk with an Ecker — as an equal?"

"An EQUAL!" Staffa was shocked. "Don't let Mother hear you talking like that!"

Jane was starting to be irritated. "You're being really funny about this, Staffa. I can't believe you've never had a real conversation with an Ecker — don't you have a maid?"

"Yes," Staffa said, "but not a girl like Twilly. My maid is called Mrs. Ingry, and she's older than Mother."

Jane suddenly saw how lonely Staffa's life had been, and stopped being annoyed with her. "You know what," she said, "you should just try spending a little time with Twilly and me. And then you'll see how sweet she is — and the three of us could have so much fun!"

"Certainly not."

"Just half an hour!"

"Oh, all right!" snapped Staffa. "But I'm only doing it because I'm bored!"

That afternoon, Jane, Staffa and Twilly met in Jane's bedroom. And at first, it was very awkward. Twilly could not forget that Staffa was a princess, and Staffa could not forget that Twilly was a servant. But Twilly was a naturally friendly person, and Staffa hungered for friends, and they gradually relaxed.

"I owe you an apology, Jane," Staffa said later. "I was wrong. Twilly's lovely. I didn't know an Ecker could be so lovely, because I've never made friends with one before."

That was the first of many long, happy afternoons. While the guns boomed outside, they all sat on Jane's bed, eating honey cake and drinking a local brew called Buttercup Yar (a little like cola, with a tang of licorice). Sometimes Staffa and Jane told Twilly about the Boy Garden. Twilly loved hearing about Jane's brothers. She knew all about large families because she had five sisters.

"There's Narcas, Pippock, Slingy, Hatbat, Toom — and me. I'm the youngest. The big girls try to boss me around."

Jane grinned. "You should see my big brothers."

"Martin, Dan and Jon," Twilly said. "Don't your brothers have funny names?"

With her triangular mouth hanging open, she listened to Jane and Staffa's stories about DVDs, cars, videos, Playstations and airplanes. None of these things could be found in the kingdom of Eck.

"We do have a sort of electricity," Staffa said. "Powered by burning moss. And there's a sort of marsh gas that lights the streets in town. But they both give very poor light."

"And they both cost a lot of money," Twilly said. "Most of us Eckers rely on beeswax candles."

"This is why bee farming is so important to our economy," Staffa said. "The bees make most of our light, and all of our sugar."

Jane asked, "How did the bees get here?"

"King Harpong the Bee Lover brought a herd through the box about two hundred years ago." Staffa said. "I have to learn all these facts and figures in my lessons — but I'm never allowed to see things for myself."

Twilly told them of the heroic beemen, who lived out on the wild hillside on the bee farms. The beemen managed herds of enormous bees and harvested their wax and honey, and they were widely admired for their toughness. Twilly's sister Pippock was a cook on a bee farm, and she was soon going to marry one of the beemen. It was a "fine match," Twilly said. The beeman's job was so hard and dangerous that the wages were very high.

"What about real sugar?" Jane asked. "I mean, sugar that doesn't come from honey, like in my world."

Twilly and Staffa looked at each other uneasily. Staffa's white cheeks turned a little pink.

"Sugar from your world is almost priceless here," Staffa said. "Unfortunately, my mother is absolutely addicted to the stuff. And I'm afraid she doesn't care how she gets it."

Jane remembered the chocolate truffle. "I suppose Prockwald buys the stuff in my world, and leaves it outside the box," she said. "And then someone comes out to fetch it."

"She sends the army," Staffa said. "And it's very difficult, dangerous work — imagine the number of men it takes to haul in a Mars Bar. They're constantly being killed by the gulls."

"The queen keeps most of her sugary things to eat herself," Twilly said. "But she sells the rest. My mam comes up to the palace to buy it — she's a master sugarsmith."

There was a busy city beyond the walls of the palace. Staffa had only seen the rooftops of this city. She had never visited its narrow streets. She listened, enthralled, as Twilly talked of her home.

Twilly's dad worked as a "slug tanner." He treated the tough skins of slugs, which were used to make waterproof cloaks. Jane supposed this must be like leather in our world. His daughters Toom and Hatbat worked with him (Hatbat was the one who had been whipped for screaming). They had a little house in the heart of the city's Slug District.

"Twilly," Staffa said one afternoon, "I'd so love to see your home! Couldn't you take us to see it?"

Twilly was shocked. "Lawks, NO! The queen would have a fit! You're not allowed to mingle with Ecker folk — and neither's Miss Jane."

"But we wouldn't be mingling, we'd only be visiting. And nobody would have to know about it."

"It can't be done, Your Highness," Twilly said firmly. "Anyway, it's too dangerous to go out at the moment, because of you-know-what."

Right on cue, there was a loud explosion outside.

Staffa groaned. "You're quite right — it's a nutty idea. This revolution is so boring, it's obviously driving me crazy."

"Oh, it never lasts for long," Twilly said bracingly. "The queen arrests a few, and she hangs a few, and then the rest of the troublemakers run away to the hills."

Once again, Staffa's thin white cheeks turned pink. She blurted out, "I know what you're both thinking. And you're quite right — now that I've got to know Twilly, I can see more clearly what I could never admit before. This is a terrible government, and my mother is a worse dictator than Harpong the Ghastly." She glared at Jane. "Why on earth are you laughing?"

"Sorry — who was Harpong the Ghastly?"

Staffa relaxed into a smile. "A medieval warlord — the last of the purely elven kings before the box came into being. He was a ghastly person. He invented a special dance for doing on his enemies' graves. And Mother is exactly like him." She took a defiant swig of her Buttercup Yar. "Twilly, I don't blame you Eckers for having revolutions. If I were an Ecker, I'd do it myself!"

Jane cheered.

Twilly looked frightened, and whispered, "Careful, Your Highness! It's not safe to speak your mind 'round here!" She looked at Staffa thoughtfully, as if trying to make up her mind about something. "Look, I've had an idea. Why don't you and Jane visit my sister Narcas?"

"Oh, that would be lovely — and Jane would find it fascinating — but dare we risk it?" Staffa was pale and eager. "Dare we?"

Twilly jumped off the bed. "Come on, nobody will see us."

She led them out through the servants' door of the room. Jane had never seen the servants' part of the palace. They hurried through a maze of bare, dusty corridors. Instead of pictures, there were notices — QUIET! YOU CAN BE HEARD IN THE THRONE ROOM! NO LAUGHING! NO HARD BOOTS BEYOND THIS POINT!

Staffa said, "We're going to have tea with the old princess."

"Who?"

"The oldest member of the royal family — well, not really royal. She's a human."

Jane was very interested, and a little uneasy. "You said there weren't any humans here."

"Officially, she doesn't exist," Staffa said. "To tell the truth, Mother never really liked her." Wary of saying any-more, she put her fingers to her lips and signaled to Jane to walk faster.

They hurried through miles of dingy corridors. They climbed miles of winding stone steps. The palace was so enormous that it took the three of them more than half an hour to reach the top of the turret where the old princess had her "secret" apartments.

Twilly rapped a secret signal on the door. An older Ecker girl, with bedspring curls just like Twilly's, opened the door. She beamed when she saw them.

"Look who it is! Oh, she will be pleased to see you!" She curtseyed to Jane. "How do you do, madam. I'm

Narcas, the old princess's personal maid. We don't get many visitors."

"It's quite safe," Twilly assured her. She said it again, nodding at Narcas in a meaningful way. "Quite safe!"

A very old, quavering voice said, "Is that my little Twilly?"

"Yes, madam darling," said Twilly. "And I brought the princess."

"Staffa?" The old voice sounded overjoyed. "Really? Oh, what a splendid surprise!"

Jane found herself in a corner of the palace that was a piece of England. The old princess's sitting room was stuffed with cozy human rugs, pictures and knick-knacks, and it reminded Jane strongly of her grandma's bungalow in Peterborough.

The old princess sat in an armchair beside the gas fire. She was very, very old, and very frail, but she smiled like a girl when she saw Staffa and Twilly. Jane saw at once that they were both extremely fond of the old lady.

Narcas smoothed the tartan rug across her knees. "And this is Miss Jane — the new girl."

Feeling shy, Jane curtseyed.

The old princess smiled. "Hello, Jane — how nice to see a new human face! Come and sit beside me, so that

I can look at you properly." She pointed to a low stool, and Jane sat down. "Gracious, how young you are! I was quite a grown-up when my husband brought me through the box."

Jane wondered who the old princess's husband had been. Was she the grandmother of Staffa and Quarley, or the great-grandmother?

"It took me some time to get used to the kingdom of Eck," said the old princess. "But I was in love, which made it easier. And I had a nice little maid to cheer me up — the granny of these two sweet sisters. Have you seen her lately, Twilly?"

"Yes, madam," Twilly said. "I popped into the Old Servants' Home on my last day off, and she's ever so well. She won the sack-race at sports day."

"Oh, that is nice. Shall we have some tea? And Jane might like to see some of the things I brought with me from my world. I wasn't supposed to bring anything, of course — it had to come through bit by bit, and my mother-in-law was very cross with she found out. But my dear husband insisted. He wanted me to be as comfortable as possible."

Narcas and Twilly set out the tea things, very quickly and neatly. There was a china tea set patterned with roses, a small jug of something that looked like milk and a plate of fairy cupcakes (Jane tasted one of these, and found it nothing like a cupcake, but pleasantly chewy). The five of them sat cozily around a small table. It was peaceful. They were at the top of the highest tower, and could hardly hear the guns.

Staffa asked, "May we see your Special Book? Jane would love it."

The old princess chuckled kindly. "Oh, I guessed you'd want to see that — you've always adored it. Narcas, would you bring it, dear?"

Narcas brought her a very old photograph album, covered with cracked red leather.

"They don't have photographs here," she told Jane. "Which is a pity, because there's no better way to store precious memories."

"We have videos now," Jane said. "I mean, moving pictures, with sounds."

"Goodness! There was nothing like that when I came through in 1927."

Jane tried to imagine having memories that stretched back to 1927. Even her grandma had only been a baby in those days. She stared at the black-and-white photos in the old princess's precious album. These were not very interesting — page after page of men with mustaches and ladies with big hats. Like Jane's grandma, the old princess loved to talk about people who were dead.

"That's my cousin Bruce. That's his wife, Barbara. Those are the Clapper sisters, who lived next door, just after their poodle won a prize at a dog show. And here's a snap of the poodle. Oh, what was his name?"

"Enoch," prompted Narcas. She had taken out her knitting.

"That's right, after the Enoch in the Bible who walked with God. Thank you, dear. He was a vicious little beast — quite the terror of Pangbourne." She turned a page. "And that's me, shortly after I met my dear husband."

She and Staffa exchanged private family smiles.

Jane looked curiously at the photograph. It showed a smiling young girl with short curly hair. She wore a white dress, and she was sitting in a flat boat on a river. A young man sat beside her, and he looked very like Quarles. This must be his grandfather, she thought. The family likeness was amazing. She was still staring at the photograph when the king himself walked into the room.

Staffa gave a yelp of joy and leapt up to hug him.

Jane was a little nervous, afraid that Narcas and Twilly would get into trouble. But she quickly saw that the two

Eckers were very relaxed with Quarles. Narcas dropped him a curtsey without putting down her knitting.

The old princess was radiant with happiness. "Quarley, my dear boy! First Staffa, and now this! What a day of lovely surprises!"

"I wanted you to be the first to know," Quarley said. "The revolution is over."

"Hooray," said Narcas, still knitting. "At last I can hang out some washing, and not have to worry about bullet holes."

The young king kissed the old princess. He sat down beside her and smiled at Jane. "Hello, Jane."

"Hi, Quarley — is it really over?"

"For the moment," Quarley said. "It's not the right time of year for revolutions. The trouble usually stops around Race Week, and doesn't start again till after the harvest."

"I used to adore Race Week," said the old princess. "The excitement! The parties! The dancing! Are you running a spider this year, darling?"

"Yes," Quarley said. "He's called Tornado Twenty-three. Let's hope he takes after his famous ancestor."

The princess clapped her trembling old hands. Her eyes shone with memories. "Oh, there'll never be another Tornado. The way that beast ran along the gutters!"

Quarley laughed and said he would place a bet for her. Jane saw that he was very fond of the old lady. He held her hand and encouraged her to talk about the old Pangbourne days until her voice had sunk to a whisper. Her eyelids, like white tissue paper, closed over her eyes. She was asleep, smiling slightly.

Quarley went through the maze of servants' corridors with the girls. Before he left them outside Jane's bedroom, her muttered, "Mother must never find out about this. She doesn't like us visiting Norah."

SILVER THREADS
AMONG THE GOLD

JANE AND STAFFA WERE IN HIGH SPIRITS THE NEXT
morning. The revolution was over, and Staffa had
promised to take Jane swimming. The sun shone. They
were both impatient to get out into the fresh air. Outside
the window of the breakfast parlor, the gardens looked
beautiful — just like the painted gardens on the box.

Queen Matilda was also very cheerful. Her black hair
was in curlers, and her face was covered with a stiff green
paste. "It's to make my skin soft for tonight," she explained, her mouth full of fried slug. "And I'll be spending the rest of the day having my bosom ironed."

Jane hid a snort of laughter. She didn't know you could iron bosoms.

The queen didn't seem to have noticed. "Tonight is the greatest occasion in our social calendar — the Race Week Ball. Thank goodness we were able to crush that pesky revolution."

"We're going to the waterfall," Staffa said. "But don't worry — we'll be back in plenty of time."

"Please see that you are, dear. This will be Jane's first ball, and I want her to look very special." She smiled hugely at Jane. A blob of green paste dropped off the end of her nose and plopped into her plate.

"Thank you, Your Majesty," Jane said. She was going to a real ball, in a real palace. It was a little scary, and almost unbearably exciting.

The gardens around the palace were a good distraction from the excitement. Directly after breakfast, Jane, Staffa and Twilly ran into the open air, like three corks shooting out of three champagne bottles. They had to walk slowly at first, because Twilly was carrying a rug, a picnic basket, an umbrella and the slugskin bag that contained their swimming things.

As soon as they were out of sight of the palace, however, Staffa said, "Give me the picnic basket, and Jane — you take the bag."

Twilly was shocked. "No, Your Highness! That wouldn't be right! And if anyone sees us — "

"Nobody will see us," Staffa said firmly, wrenching the picnic basket out of her hands.

Jane grabbed the slugskin bag. "Come on, Twilly — if you want to be a good servant, here's an order for you — stop being a servant."

This made Twilly and Staffa laugh. Swinging their bags, the three of them gave themselves up to the joy of being outside. The palace gardens were very beautiful (despite the bomb damage that dozens of Ecker gardeners were clearing up) and rather strange. There were trees and shrubs and smooth lawns that looked just the same as they would to full-grown humans in the normal human world. But there were several clumps of enormous dandelions, and shady forest glades of forget-me-nots; and they passed two gardeners chopping down a mushroom the size of an oak tree.

Maybe the box world can't quite keep out the human world, Jane thought, and there are patches where it shows through, as if the skin were wearing too thin. Or maybe it's the box itself that muddles things up.

After about an hour of hot walking, they came to a natural pool that was hidden in a grove of forget-me-nots, with a little waterfall cascading down from the rocks on one side — Jane thought it looked delicious, and she couldn't wait to get into the silvery water. The three of them changed into their swimsuits — bulky, old-fashioned things that covered their legs down to the knees.

Jane loved swimming, and this pool was bliss — she could have fooled about under the waterfall all day. By the time they climbed out and ate their picnic, the three girls were wrinkled like prunes. The sun shone, and the snail cheese sandwiches tasted wonderful. Staffa had forgotten she was a princess, and Twilly had forgotten she was a servant. Jane had forgotten that they were anything but three normal girls.

"Ooh, look!" Twilly squealed suddenly while they were packing up the picnic. "This is a sight you must see, Jane! You can't beat it for excitement and handsomeness — a beeman out pollening!"

Jane thought at first that a small airplane, with a loud, buzzing engine, was flying towards them. As it came closer, she saw that it was a huge bee. Its wings sliced the air in a metallic blur. Its face was a menacing mask carved from what looked like black plastic. It carried a large sack on each of its back legs. Unlike any bee in the human world, it wore a harness and a saddle. A brawny young Ecker man rode on its back. He swerved the bee away from them in a showing-off way that made Twilly giggle. "Oh, don't you think he's handsome?"

Staffa laughed, and said she thought he fancied himself enough for all of them. "Come on, we'd better get back to the castle."

"But the ball's not for hours!" Jane protested. "Couldn't we have one more swim?"

"Sorry," Staffa said with a sigh. "Preparing for the Race Week Ball is a very serious business, and it's supposed to take a long time. Look at Mother — she'll be clapped in those bosom irons for at least two hours, and then she'll have her hair stretched."

"Cheer up, Jane," said Twilly. "It's the biggest night of the year, and all the very grandest people in the land will be there. Oh, it's a wonderful spectacle! I'll be watching from the servants' gallery, and I'll be wearing a blue dress and my new pink apron."

"What shall I wear?" Jane asked. "The yellow again?"

"Lawk, no! You wait and see."

THE PALACE WAS BUSTLING WITH PREPARATIONS FOR THE ball. They found servants spreading purple carpet over the cobblestones in the courtyard, and carrying large tubs of flowers into the ballroom. More servants hammered at a great platform in the ballroom. There were servants carrying thrones, servants polishing the stair rails, servants hanging peculiar metal cages from the high ceiling — servants swarming everywhere.

Twilly ran Jane a warm bath, full of floating petals. When Jane had dried herself with a towel as soft as thistledown, it was time to put on the dress. Twilly washed her hands twice before taking Jane's ball dress out of the wardrobe. She held it in her arms, and both girls stared at it in silence — until Jane said, "I think that's the loveliest dress I've ever seen."

It was of the purest white, with a huge skirt and short sleeves, embroidered all over with shimmering silver stuff that gleamed and glittered in the feeble electric light.

"It's made of cobweb," Twilly whispered. "The queen ordered it for you two weeks ago."

She brushed Jane's long red hair, and dressed it with jewels. She pulled long white gloves over Jane's bare arms, and buckled white shoes onto her feet.

Jane stared at herself in the long mirror. She didn't look like herself at all. She wished Mom and Dad could see her. She looked like every girl's secret idea of a princess.

"Oh, Jane!" sighed Twilly. "You're as beautiful as Migorn!"

Jane knew this was a great compliment — Twilly adored Migorn. She asked, "Will Migorn be at the ball?"

"Lawk, no," Twilly said. "Theater people don't mix with royalty. But you might get to see her at the Races."

There was a knock at the door. Jane thought it would be Staffa, but it was Captain Hooter — very splendid in his purple dress uniform, so crusted with gold that you could hardly see the purple.

He had come to escort Jane down to the ballroom.

Twilly gave her a friendly kiss. "Have a wonderful time — I'll be watching!"

Jane felt a little awkward with Captain Hooter, but she enjoyed the way her white skirts billowed around her as they walked in silence through the endless corridors. After all the boredom and gunfire of the revolution, it lifted her heart to hear the buzzing sound of the orchestra, and the roar of a crowd from behind the doors of the palace ballroom.

Captain Hooter threw open the doors. In a very loud voice, he announced, "The Lady Jane!"

Instantly, all the music and the talking stopped. Jane found herself staring at several hundred Eckers, all staring at her. There was a sudden movement like wind over a cornfield as they all bowed or curtseyed.

Jane was very embarrassed, and rather alarmed — why on earth were they doing this?

To her relief, the talking and music started again immediately afterwards. Once everyone had stopped taking notice of her, Jane could look around. She saw that the ballroom blazed with light. Besides the feeble lamps, there were large, flickering, shifting orbs of light in cages that hung from the ceiling.

"They're fireflies, madam," Captain Hooter explained. "They were captured in your world a hundred years ago by King Harpong the Innovator. They're specially bred to light large spaces."

The ballroom windows stood open. More firefly cages glowed in the trees outside, like Japanese lanterns. The ballroom and the gardens were thronged with the cream of Ecker society, in splendid dresses and uniforms. Jane had never seen anything so beautiful in her life. This was a scene straight out of a fairy tale.

The royal family sat on a low platform. Jane was surprised and pleased to see that the old princess was with them. She was beside the young king, holding his hand tightly and looking very happy — Jane guessed that she had not been out of her secret room for ages. She wore a gray satin gown and a small, glittering crown, and she smiled when she saw Jane.

"Oh, Jane, my dear, how thrilling — your first Race Week Ball! And you look so pretty! Doesn't she, Quarley?"

"Very pretty," the king said, giving Jane a friendly smile. "I hope you'll save me the first dance."

Jane said, "I don't know any dances."

"Don't worry. This one couldn't be easier." He lowered his voice. "Sorry about the bowing and curtseying — I think Mother must have gotten a bit carried away."

"I thought they'd all made a mistake," Jane said, giggling. "Who do they think I am?"

Staffa said, "The Eckers seem to think you're a visitor from a foreign government." She was wearing a long dress of sky blue velvet and a small crown that blazed with diamonds. Jane saw that she was uneasy about something — why did she keep frowning to herself, and glancing suspiciously at her mother?

"Jane!" boomed the queen. "You are simply divine! Don't sit down for a minute, dear — let the Eckers see you properly. They're terribly nosy creatures; even the posh

ones." She wore an amazing crown of knobbly gold that
looked like plumbing. Her bright green dress had a very
low neck, to show off her ironed bosom, which was as
hard and white and shiny as a new sink.

Jane dropped her a deep curtsey, to hide an attack of
nervous giggles.

The queen's voice suddenly dropped to an exaggerated
whisper. "Keep smiling, Jane. We have had some unset-
tling news. The upper classes can no longer be trusted. My
spies inform me that there is a leading terrorist working in
my own aristocracy! The ingratitude! I wish I could arrest
them all, but there isn't the prison space."

The band began to play. It was a strange, mourning,
whining sound, like gnats on a summer evening. Quarley
stood up and bowed to Jane. The crowd of Eckers broke
into a round of applause. Jane's cheeks were hot. Never
in her life had she felt so embarrassed. Everyone in the
huge ballroom was suddenly silent, and staring at her.

The old princess kindly patted her hand. "I know just
how you feel," she said softly. "I was nervous too. But you
mustn't worry — these people have very good hearts!"

"Do I have to?" Jane whispered to Quarley. "I'm lousy
at dancing — my dad says I've got two left feet."

Quarley smiled — he was unusually cheerful tonight.

"You'll soon get the hang of it." He led Jane to the middle of the dance floor. "Don't mind them staring at you. They don't mean any harm."

"But what if I fall over, or something?"

"You can if you like," said Quarley. "They'll only copy you. That's the thing about being royal — whatever you do, it's always right. Look." He suddenly kicked up one of his legs. Everyone in the crowd immediately did the same.

Jane couldn't help laughing — the Eckers looked so silly, sometimes kicking each other by mistake. Many of them were laughing, and the old princess clapped her hands delightedly. Jane began to think this might be fun. The dance was called the Race Week Gallop. Quarley and Staffa showed her the movements, which were mainly twirling around very fast, and stamping the floor very hard. The pace was furious. Part of the dance was a race around the floor with all the other couples. Jane twirled and stamped until she was breathless and her hair was falling down on one side.

The dance ended with a round of applause. Jane collapsed into the chair next to the old princess.

"That was perfectly brilliant!" declared the old princess. With a shaking hand, she tidied Jane's hair. "Oh, look — there's my little Twilly, and dear Narcas, up in the gallery! Let's give them a wave."

Jane looked up at the servants' gallery. The bedspring curls of Twilly and Narcas bounced right at the front of a crowd of palace servants. They were eating cake and talking nonstop. When Jane and the old princess waved to them, Twilly was so excited that she waved her slice of cake, and dropped it into the helmet of a soldier standing below.

"I wish they could be down here with us," Jane said.

The old princess chuckled. "I think they're having much more fun up there. Narcas will be full of stories tomorrow."

Captain Hooter came to the royal platform. "Excuse me, Your Majesty." He bowed to the queen. "The Dancing Orphans are here."

Queen Matilda scowled. "Who invited the Dancing Orphans?" She shook with fury. "Tell them to go away at once!"

"Don't do any such thing, Hooter," Quarley said sternly. "The orphans must have heard that the princess was going to be here tonight. They only want to pay their respects."

"I don't trust those orphans!" hissed the queen. "I daresay they've all got bombs hidden up their skirts!"

"Mother, don't be silly — they're children!"

"They catch them young, you know!"

"It's too late to turn them away," Quarley said, "unless you want another revolution."

"Oh, very well!" snapped the queen, hideous with fury. "Hooter, let in the little squirts!"

Jane couldn't imagine why she was in such a state — especially when Staffa explained to her that the Dancing Orphans came from an orphanage that had been founded by the old princess. What was wrong with that?

"She taught them to dance, and they've had a dance troupe ever since," Staffa said.

The ballroom fell silent. The crowds stepped back, to make a large space in the middle of the floor. A little Ecker girl, dressed in a pink tutu, tripped into the space. She carried an odd-looking musical instrument, a little like a small harp. Her delicate hands plucked at the strings, and the air was filled with a twanging that sounded strange yet sweet.

Ten little girls, also in pink tutus, and wearing the wings of butterflies, fluttered out with wonderful grace, standing on the very tips of their long feet. Their legs were long, and their feet were very flexible. They did not dance like humans exactly, yet there was something enchanting in the sight of them. Jane thought she had never seen anything so close to real fairies. They shimmered and spun, as light as gossamer, and finished their dance by sinking into deep curtseys at the feet of the old princess.

"Thank you, my dears," the old princess said. "You all dance beautifully!"

The little girl with the harp walked up to the king. With a curtsey, she gave the harp to him. The Eckers, who had been watching in silence, broke into murmurs.

Someone bold shouted, "Sing, Your Majesty!"

A few people tried, and failed, to start a round of applause. Everyone was staring at the queen.

"Oh, I see what's going on!" fumed Queen Matilda. "Don't you dare sing, Quarley. Your father used to sing all the time. It was just plain embarrassing if you ask me."

"I'm not asking you," said Quarley. He bent down towards the old princess, and the expression on his stern young face was very tender. "Would you like me to sing?"

The dim eyes of the old princess shone with happiness. "Oh, darling, I'd love it."

"You'll remember this. It comes from the happy old Pangbourne days." He struck a silvery chord and began to sing, as if he and the old princess were the only people in the room:

Darling, I am growing old,
Silver threads among the gold
Shine upon my brow today,
Life is fading fast away.

But, my darling, you will be
Always young and fair to me!

The old princess listened with a dreamy smile. The years seemed to peel away from her. How pretty she was, Jane thought.

The last notes faded away into silence.

"Thank you," the old princess said. With a frail hand, she wiped her wrinkled cheek where a tear had fallen. "That brought back some lovely memories. You've made me feel quite young again."

Quarley leaned down close to the old princess, and Jane heard him murmur, "Always young and fair to me!"

Queen Matilda coughed irritably. "Is it finished? Good. Let's have more dancing."

The crowd of Eckers stood absolutely still and absolutely silent.

"What's the matter with you?" shouted the queen. "Start enjoying yourselves at once!"

A man's voice shouted, "Long live the old princess!"

There was a great gasp of horror. Then another voice took up the cry: "Long live the old princess!"

The Eckers began to clap — just a few of them at first, then more and more, until the whole ballroom was clapping and cheering. Up in the servants' gallery, Narcas and Twilly cheered with all their might.

"Captain Hooter!" roared the queen, "this is sedition and insurrection and sheer CHEEK! Arrest as many people as possible!"

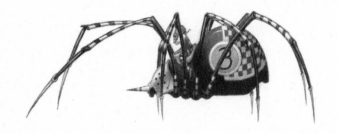

A DAY AT THE RACES

"GOOD MORNING, YOUR JANESHIP. IT'S A LOVELY DAY, and you're off to the Races. You're to wear the short blue dress with a matching bonnet."

"Morning, Twilly." Jane opened her eyes. Twilly stood beside her bed, holding out a sky blue dress. She was doing her best to smile, but her triangular face was blotchy and swollen with crying. She looked as if she had been crying for hours.

"Twilly? What's the matter?" Jane scrambled out of bed. "What's happened?"

"Nothing," Twilly said miserably. "I'm fine. Nothing's the matter."

Jane grabbed one of her hands. "Something's wrong — you can't hide it from me. Why are you crying?"

Twilly said, "I'm not crying!" — and immediately broke down into frightened sobs. "Oh, what shall I do? Don't notice me!"

"I can't help noticing you — oh, please tell me what's wrong! I might be able to help!" Jane put her arms around her weeping little maid and hugged her until her sobs died down. Then she made Twilly sit in the soft armchair while she poured them both a refreshing glass of Buttercup Yar.

Twilly blew her red nose. "You mustn't say it was me who told you. I'm not supposed to know until the official announcement."

"Know what?"

"It's the old princess," Twilly whispered. "She . . . she's dead!"

How dark the room looked suddenly, in spite of the sunbeams that danced around it.

"What? But . . . but . . . she can't be! She was so well last night!"

"Yes, and she went to bed as happy as anything — but when Narcas took in her breakfast this morning — " Twilly swallowed another sob. " — Narcas said she was smiling just like an angel, but she was as dead as the queen's dead heart. You humans do wear out so quick!"

Jane felt her own eyes filling with tears. It was dreadful to think of that sweet old lady dying so far from home. "Poor Narcas," she said. "And poor you — I know how much you both loved her."

"That we did, Your Janeship. Just as if she'd been our own granny. You can't think how kind she was to us — she always said we were her children, because she didn't have any of her own."

Jane thought about what happened at home, in England, when a royal person died. There was bound to be a big funeral, with sad music and everyone wearing deepest black. "Well, we can't go to the Races now," she said. "The old bag had her bosoms ironed for nothing."

"Shhh!" Twilly was scared. "The racing is carrying on as usual — the queen says there's not to be any mentioning of the old princess!"

Jane was shocked. "She expects us to dress up and have a good time? That's horrible!"

Twilly whispered, "I think so too, but we can't disobey. The queen's in a terrible mood because of what happened at the ball."

After the cheers for the old princess, thirty people had been arrested — in full evening dress — and led away by soldiers. It had been impossible to enjoy the ball after that.

"We weren't the only Eckers who loved her," whispered Twilly. "And loving the princess is the same as hating the queen. Now, please put on your dress for the Races, Your Janeship! I have to take you down to the breakfast barge."

"The — what?"

"We must be quick." Twilly blew her nose again and sprang to her feet. She picked up the blue dress. She would not allow Jane to ask any more questions.

Because she did not want to get Twilly into trouble, Jane put on the blue dress, and a huge blue bonnet the size of a dustbin.

"I look absolutely stupid," she said scornfully, frowning at her reflection. She was starting to think she'd had enough of girls' clothes — especially when they made her look like Little Bo Peep.

Twilly (looking fearfully around her all the time) led Jane through a maze of corridors she had not seen before. They looked like all the other corridors in the castle, but the pictures were different. They passed several pale, empty squares of wall.

Jane asked, "What used to be here? Why were they taken away?"

"Your Janeship, I beg you!" hissed Twilly. "These are the king's apartments, and they were pictures of the old princess — now please stop asking questions!"

"But why did the queen hate her so much that she — "

A terrible voice suddenly shouted, "I don't know why I bother!"

Jane and Twilly jumped like rabbits. It was the voice of the queen, ranting at someone behind a nearby door.

"I'm utterly fed up with the pair of you! You're ungrateful, you're lazy, you're selfish — "

Twilly tugged urgently at Jane's dress. Jane refused to move — she wanted to listen.

Staffa's voice said, "Mother, how could you? How could you do such a thing?"

"I had to act quickly," said the queen.

"Why?" Staffa cried. "She wasn't doing any harm!"

"Oh, yes she was! She undermined my authority from the moment she came to this castle!"

"Only because she made the people love her! You couldn't stand that, could you, Mother? You were jealous of her."

Twilly tugged at Jane's skirt so hard that she almost tore it. Jane shook her hand off impatiently. They were talking about the old princess and she was determined to find out why Queen Matilda had hated her.

The queen said, "Oh, stop whining. Quarley's not the only one to make sacrifices. I don't do this sort of thing for fun, you know. Do you think I *enjoyed* killing her? I thought we settled all this sentimental nonsense when I killed your father."

Jane felt sick. The horror of it took a moment to sink in. It was incredible — but in her bones she felt it was true. The queen had murdered the old princess. She had murdered her own husband. She wasn't even ashamed. She was as wicked as an old witch in a fairy tale, and Jane was sure she had a witch's talent for magic — how else, after all, did you explain a whole world in a painted box? She'd told herself the magic in this place must be good magic. Now she wasn't so sure.

The queen said, "I really haven't time to worry about Quarley's so-called broken heart. And if you don't stop that sniveling, Miss Staffa, you'll be sent off to join him."

Twilly whispered, "Now you see why it's better not to notice — it's dangerous to know too much."

Limp with shock, Jane allowed Twilly to drag her away.

Clutching Jane's hand, Twilly led her down some stone steps and pushed open a heavy wooden door. Jane blinked in bright sunlight. She was on the bank of a wide canal. A long, flat barge was on the water, decorated with flags and ribbons that fluttered in the summer breeze. A band played on the deck. There was a large buffet table laden with food

— the centerpiece was an entire slug, roasted whole and garnished with the seeds of forget-me-nots.

The fresh air cleared Jane's head. She did not want to stay in this awful country, with the witch-like queen who talked so casually about killing people. She wanted to go home. But how was that to be done? She was impatient to talk to Staffa.

The band, which had been tootling out the hits of Migorn, suddenly switched to a stately march. The queen (in bright red, with a tall hat like a mailbox) stomped onto the barge, followed by Staffa and Captain Hooter. Staffa was deathly pale. She would not speak to Jane, or even look at her.

"Well, Jane," said the queen, "I'm afraid Quarley won't be joining us today. He's gone to spend a few days at our hunting lodge in the hills — such a healing, restful place." She frowned down at Jane. "Your dress clashes dreadfully with mine. Hooter — keep her away from me."

"Yes, Your Majesty." Captain Hooter gently pushed Jane to the other side of the barge.

Jane was only too pleased to keep away from the murdering queen. She went up to Staffa — but Staffa hurried away from her. What was going on? Why was Staffa avoiding her? And why had Quarley suddenly gone to the hunting lodge, on the most important day in the social calendar?

She sat on a rather uncomfortable gold chair. Twilly stood behind her, holding a parasol over her head against the sun. The barge set off very slowly. The canal ran through the narrow streets of the city, and she caught tantalizing glimpses of colorful houses and neat shops. Beyond the city, they went through meadows and woods. They passed farmhouses — long buildings made of soil, with flowers growing on the roofs.

At about eleven in the morning, the royal barge arrived at the race course. This was packed with crowds of Eckers in holiday clothes. There were bright little food stalls selling Buttercup Yar and Haw-haw tea and what looked like hard little pies with shiny black crusts. Three bands were playing at once, on strange, buzzing instruments that sounded like insects. It was a cheerful scene, but if you looked closely, nobody was having a good time. The Eckers looked sulky, or scared, or very sad. A few were crying silently into their pies.

And they stared at Jane, in a way that made her very uncomfortable.

"What's the matter?" she whispered to Twilly. "Why is everyone gawking at me?"

"I don't know, Your Janeship," Twilly whispered. "But something's going on, I can tell — if I get a chance, I'll slip into the crowd and find out what it is."

"Come, Jane!" boomed the queen, "let us go to the enclosure, to see the spiders — you can get rid of your maid."

Twilly curtseyed, winked at Jane and trotted away into the crowd.

"Don't stand too close to me, dear," the queen said. "Ugh, that blue! Would you like a gubb?"

"A — what?" Jane was still following Twilly's curly head through the throng of people.

"Rather vulgar food, I know," the queen went on, "but very tasty. Hooter! Fetch us a couple of good fat gubbs!"

"Yes, Your Majesty." Captain Hooter pushed through the crowd around one of the stalls selling the hard pies and bought two. They were wrapped in paper and roughly the size of teacups. A hot, heavy gubb was put into Jane's hand. She was shocked to discover that it was not a pie, but a sort of barbecued black beetle. The queen picked off the legs of her gubb and crunched them like pretzels. With her finger, she scooped the gubb out of its shell, swallowed it whole and threw the shell on the ground — which, Jane now saw, was covered with gubb shells. She felt sick.

"Don't you like it?" demanded the queen. "Give it to me." She gulped Jane's gubb and threw the shell over her shoulder. "Now, let's go and admire those spiders!"

The racing spiders were kept in a large enclosure, behind a tall fence. Jane knew people who were scared of normal-size spiders, and thought how terrified they would have been of these gigantic beasts. Dozens of huge spiders were pushing against one another and trying to scuttle into corners. Their bodies were blotchy. Their legs were long and tough and hairy. They had dreadful, eyeless faces and big, puckered mouths. Each spider wore a saddle of different colored slugskin and had an Ecker jockey crouched on its back.

"Tornado Twenty-three is the one with the blue saddle," the queen told Jane. "He belongs to Quarley. My spider wears the red saddle, and her name is Deathlegs. I'm extremely proud of her — she's killed four husbands, and she's only three months old." (Jane, with a deep shudder, thought that Deathlegs and her owner had quite a lot in common).

Queen Matilda bent down and took something from a bucket on the ground — a large chunk of something black that dripped unpleasantly. She tossed it to Deathlegs.

"A bit of fly's leg," she explained, wiping her hands on the hair of a nearby servant. "Spider racing has a glorious history in our country, Jane. It was introduced by one of my ancestors, King Harpong the Wasteful."

There were other people in the enclosure — stable

workers, jockeys and the owners of spiders. Yet the mood was sober and sad. Nobody was having a good time, except the queen.

"Jane — don't stare at the Eckers, dear. It only encourages them."

"I'm sorry, Your Majesty," Jane said, reddening. "I was just . . . thinking."

"Thinking about what, dear?" the queen leaned down towards Jane.

Jane felt the queen's curiosity like tentacles trying to slither into her mind. She stammered, "I — I — was just thinking how many of your kings were called Harpong."

"Oh, yes, dear." This feeble invention seemed to satisfy the queen. "They were all called Harpong — until the reign of my grandfather, King Harpong the Unpopular."

She turned her back on the spiders and marched off to the Royal Hut beside the winning post. Jane went after her, looking at the ground to avoid the stares of the crowd. In spite of everything being so strange and scary, she couldn't help being interested. It was such a lively, colorful scene — the bands played and the starting horns blew and the spiders stamped and snorted.

The sight of the giant spiders scuttling around the course was astonishing — simply astonishing. Imagine it, if you can. Jane wished her brothers could see it. The spiders ran around a series of gutters and drainpipes, and two dangerous obstacles that looked like huge plugholes.

"COME ON, DEATHLEGS!" roared the queen.

The first race was called the Batsindo Gong (named after the famous jockey in the queen's song). Deathlegs won, and the queen was so excited that it took her a few minutes to notice the silence of the crowd.

"Dear me, they're sulky," she remarked, busily counting her winnings (small, stiff bills like train tickets). "I acted just in time."

Jane looked around the Royal Hut, hoping to see Staffa, but the only other people, besides herself and the queen, were a crowd of Ecker courtiers — who all stared back at her, in eerie silence. She was alone with a murderer, and it made her so nervous that she had to put down her cup of Buttercup Yar because her hands were shaking.

The queen moved her chair closer, and lowered her booming voice. "You know, Jane, there's a lot of ingratitude in this kingdom."

Feeling that the queen expected some kind of answer, Jane said, "Oh."

"These wretched people are never satisfied! It was all that Norah's doing." (Jane remembered that Norah had been the name of the old princess). "She turned herself into a figurehead, you see, Jane — a champion of every malcontent and troublemaker in the land. Did you know that the most dangerous group of revolutionaries actually call themselves 'the Norahs' after her? Oh, yes! They think they're a secret society — but I'll find the ringleaders!"

"Oh," Jane said again.

"My big mistake," said the queen, "was to let her move about freely amongst the people. I should have kept her under house arrest from the very beginning! Well, that's a mistake I won't make again. Do you hear me, Jane? Do you understand?"

Jane didn't really understand a word of it, but the queen loomed over her so forbiddingly that she stammered, "Y-yes, Your Majesty."

The queen took a large bite of the lump of chocolate on her plate. She smiled, and said, "I've told you all about my little hunting lodge in the mountains, haven't I? Really, at this time of year, it's a delightful spot! I've decided that it would be nice for all of us to visit Quarley up there for a couple of months."

Jane said, "I suppose I'll be going home, then."

"Home, Jane?"

"I mean, if you and Staffa are going to see Quarley — well — "

"Oh, you're coming too, dear."

"But — Your Majesty," Jane said carefully, "I can't stay for a couple of months — I have to get home in a couple of weeks! We're going camping, and then I'm starting my new school."

"Please don't worry, Jane," said the queen. Her voice was light, but her eyes gleamed with menace. "I shall see to your education."

A terrible coldness settled around Jane. "I think I'd better go home soon," she said bravely. "To my world."

"Oh, you'll have forgotten all about that other world in a few weeks. Think of it as a dream."

"But it's not a dream!" Jane cried. "You can't keep me here! My parents will be worried about me!"

"On the contrary," said the queen, "they'll be pleased that you're off their hands — they clearly can't afford you."

This was a horrible thing to say. Jane held up her head proudly. "They're expecting me to come home."

"At the end of this month," said the queen, "your parents will hear that you have been killed in a helicopter crash."

"*What?*"

"I did the same thing with that Norah woman," said the queen, calmly chewing chocolate. "Except that helicopters hadn't been invented in those days — it had to be a freak carriage accident. It's the kindest way to do it. You wouldn't want your parents to waste their time searching for you, would you?"

Jane felt as if she had been punched in the stomach. She was breathless with shock and fear. The queen meant to keep her inside the box forever. Unless she escaped before the end of the month, her parents would think their only daughter was dead. But why did the coldhearted old monster of a queen want to keep her here, anyway? Jane didn't understand any of it, and didn't want to understand. This place was complicated and frightening, and all she wanted was to go home.

Captain Hooter stepped up to the queen. "Your Majesty, the entertainment is about to begin."

"Come, Jane," said the queen. "Let's show you off to the rabble."

"Show me off? What do you mean?"

"My dear child," said the queen. Her words were kind, but her voice was an icy dagger, and her eyes were flat blue discs of pure wickedness. She leaned very close to Jane. "When will you learn to stop asking these dangerous questions? Shut up and do as you're told."

Jane was very glad to be joined by Staffa. "Where have you been?" she whispered.

"I'm sorry I couldn't take care of you, Jane," Staffa said coldly. "I had to entertain some mayors from out of town."

"Staffa, why are you avoiding me?"

"You're joining us in the Royal Box," Staffa said, as if she hadn't heard. "Don't sit down until I tell you."

"Staffa!" Jane hissed. "You have to listen to me — your mother says she won't let me go home!"

"I'm afraid I'm not allowed to discuss these matters," Staffa said coldly.

"I thought I was supposed to be your best friend!"

Was it her imagination, or did she see a flicker of anxiety in Staffa's face? Before Jane could decide, she was cold again.

"Friendship is one thing," Staffa said. "Politics is quite another."

"I'm not talking about politics!" snapped Jane. "Tell me what's going on!"

Staffa's fingers suddenly grabbed Jane's wrist.

"Ow, that hurts!"

"Don't be a fool, Jane — for lawks sake, shut up!"

"Stop that whispering, you two!" called the queen. "You'll have plenty of time for girlish confidences when we're in the mountains!"

She was smiling, but the expression on her painted

face was horrible. Jane saw that Staffa was pale with fear and decided to shut up. They walked together, in prickly silence, behind the looming red form of the queen.

There was a huge red-and-white–striped tent, like the big top at a circus, next to the Royal Hut. The queen led the procession. It was a short walk, but very embarrassing for Jane. Staring Eckers surrounded them all on sides. The general mood was still sad — but there were growing mutterings of anger. People were getting bold, and making loud remarks.

"Is that her? Never. She's too small."

"She'll grow!"

"I like her hair."

"Her neck's too short."

"No, it ain't — they all got short necks."

It was a great relief to reach the tent, and climb the private wooden staircase to the Royal Box.

"This will be a treat for you, Jane," said the queen. "You're going to see Migorn."

"Really?" For a second, Jane forgot how worried she was. It would be fascinating to see the Ecker star in person. Poor Twilly would be so jealous (and where was Twilly? It was hours since she had slipped away into the crowds).

Jane gasped aloud when she stepped into the Royal Box. The huge tent held a roughly-built theater, with rows and rows of wooden seats, right up to the striped roof. She had a feverish impression of thousands of bright eyes, glittering in a wall of curious faces.

The queen stepped to the front of the box. The band in the orchestra pit played the droning national anthem. Jane noticed that there were a lot of soldiers patroling the audience, and that many people in the audience looked angry. And so few joined in the national anthem that Captain Hooter was almost singing a solo.

The queen did not seem to care about this. She sat down. Jane and Staffa sat down on either side of her. The lights in the great tent faded into comfortable darkness. To Jane's great relief, the thousands of bright eyes turned away from her to the stage. The purple curtains opened, and the audience burst into loud cheers.

"Migorn! Migorn!"

Jane was getting used to the triangular, chinless Ecker face, and she saw at once that Migorn was very pretty. She had golden curls, big, blue mouse eyes, a little round body and long skinny legs. Her feet were enormous, and very bendy. She danced as lightly and as gracefully as a hummingbird. Migorn sang her latest hit, "His Heart

Was as Big as a Beetle's Leg," in a voice that was partly human and partly like birdsong, and very sweet to hear.

> *His heart was as big as a beetle's leg*
> *And as brave as a fighting bee!*
> *He was curly*
> *And burly*
> *And I was his girly — he promised to marry me!*
> *But his mam was as fat as a beetle's bum*
> *And as mean as a wasp with a grudge!*
> *She said "No!*
> *"She's too low!*
> *"I want her to go — and you'll never get me to budge!"*

After the song, there was a sort of musical play. Migorn was a simple snail maid who fell in love with a prince. But the prince was under a terrible spell. His mother was a dragon, who kept him tied to her with invisible chains. He couldn't marry the snail maid until the chains were broken.

It was very entertaining, but Jane was uneasy. The audience was starting to get rowdy. When the hideous dragon mother appeared onstage, there were roars of laughter and many blew raspberries.

Migorn sang a song called "Let's Kill Your Mother and Get Married," and the cheers were so loud that she had to sing it three times. The last time, everyone in the audience joined the rousing chorus. Some of them stood up.

> *Let's kill your mother and get married!*
> *Let's not beat about the bush!*
> *Just get her to the top of the stairs,*
> *And give her a great big push!*
> *She's a mad old fart who's had her day,*
> *She's breaking all the furniture and getting in the way!*
> *We can't do a thing till the old dragon's dead,*
> *So let's kill your mother and get wed!*

It was only too obvious that they were angry with the queen. It could not have been more obvious if the queen herself had appeared on the stage as the dragon, and the actor who played the prince had been dressed to look like Quarley. Amazingly, however, the queen did not seem to have noticed — she even joined in the song.

"That was catchy!" she declared when the song was over.

Suddenly, the door of the Royal Box crashed open and then everything happened very fast — Jane had a nightmare impression of several figures, all shrouded in black from head to foot. All that could be seen of them was their gleaming eyes, and the steely glint of their guns.

The queen let out a blood-curdling scream, but the audience was still cheering Migorn, and no one heard. Captain Hooter was knocked unconscious by one of the figures in black.

Someone grabbed Jane roughly. A man's voice growled in her ear, "Don't struggle and don't make a noise!"

Jane was too frightened to make any kind of noise. The man in black worked very quickly. She felt her hands being tied behind her back. A gag was put around her mouth and a blindfold around her eyes. It was terrifying to feel herself so helpless.

"Hooter!" shrieked the queen's voice, mad with fury. "Get up at once! Have everyone arrested and killed! You there — take your filthy hands off the human! She's MINE, do you hear? Oh, I know who you are — I'll hunt you down and feed you to the gulls!"

Jane felt herself being heaved up over someone's shoulder. She felt herself jolting, and she heard pounding footsteps, as she was carried out of the Royal Box and down the wooden stairs.

The screams of the queen fell away behind her. She

felt fresh air on her face, then her body slammed down on a wooden floor, so hard that tears sprang to her eyes.

"Shut up and keep still," said the man's voice. "You've been captured by the Norahs!"

THE NORAHS

SHE WAS IN SOME KIND OF CLOSED CART OR VAN, jolting quickly and painfully over a very rough road. Her thoughts were a mix of confusion and terror. Who were these Norahs, and where were they taking her? What did they want with her? Was she about to be killed? Would she ever see her parents again?

Jane did not often cry, but she cried now — and it was very uncomfortable, because the tears made her blindfold damp, and she couldn't wipe her nose. After what felt like a lifetime, but was about an hour, she fell into a miserable doze.

She woke to the sound of gunfire, and screamed behind her gag. There were noises of angry voices and running feet. The van lumbered on, twisting and turning, and Jane guessed that they must be among the narrow city streets she had seen on her way to the Races. They came to a sudden stop. Jane heard the door being opened and felt cool air on her face.

A strong hand grabbed her ankle. She was pulled out of the van. There was a horrible smell in the air — like the hamburgers the twins had once left in the garage and then forgotten. Feeling light-headed and a little sick, Jane listened to the sound of the van moving away across cobblestones.

A hand took Jane's, and she felt herself being led into a room.

"Please don't be scared," a quiet, indoor voice said. "We had to grab you quickly — it was an emergency."

Someone untied Jane's hands and took off her gag. The blindfold was whisked off her eyes — and she was face-to-face with the last person in the world that she had expected to see.

She gasped. "Staffa!"

"Are you all right?"

"I don't understand," Jane said. "I thought I'd been kidnapped by the Norahs!"

Staffa smiled. "You have."

"What? Staffa, what's going on?"

"I'm one of the Norahs," Staffa said. "Sorry I couldn't tell you."

"But —" Jane said. She shook her head, trying to clear it. "But doesn't that mean you're trying to overthrow the queen?"

"Certainly," Staffa said coolly.

"She's your mother!"

Staffa's childish face was pale and stern. "She's gone too far this time, Jane. Wouldn't you want to overthrow your mother if she killed your father and sent your brother to prison?"

"Who's in prison?" Jane was struggling to keep up. "The queen said Quarley had gone to the hunting lodge."

"It's not a hunting lodge," Staffa said. "She makes me sick when she tells lies about it. It's a prison fortress in the mountains, and very few people come out alive." She took Jane's hand. "And now, as you heard, she's decided to send you there."

"A prison?" Jane was bewildered. "Why does she want to send me to prison? Does she think I've done something bad?"

"I'll explain it all later," Staffa said. "You're safe now, that's the important thing."

"You might have warned me about all this," Jane said crossly. "I didn't think I'd spend my vacation being kidnapped and hiding from the police."

"I know," Staffa said. "But please don't be angry with me — I wanted you to come so much! I've never had a friend before. Honestly, I only meant to keep you for a couple of weeks! I had no idea that Mother would hatch one of her evil plots."

"Oh, well," Jane said. She didn't want to quarrel with Staffa. She was glad that they were friends again. It made her feel much stronger. "Where are we, anyway?"

Staffa smiled. "Can't you guess from the smell? We're in the heart of the Slug District."

Jane's heart gave a leap of hope. "Oh — is this Twilly's house?"

"Yes — her father's tannery is around the back, and this is her mother's workshop. She's a master sugarsmith, as you know."

Jane's eyes became used to the shadowy darkness, and she saw that they were in a shop with long wooden counters, and racks of metal tools hung on the walls. There was a notice beside the empty window: NO SUGAR IS KEPT IN THIS SHOP OVERNIGHT. She remembered that sugar was like gold in the world of the box.

"It was Narcas who started the Norahs," Staffa's pale eyes glinted with excitement. "And now there are thousands of us! All the students at the university have joined — and the Guild of Bee Workers, the Guild of Sugarsmiths, the Guild of Slug Tanners — even some of the servants at the castle!" Staffa was obviously very proud of being a Norah. "I joined the day we had tea with the old princess. Twilly came secretly to my room that night."

"But . . . why didn't you wake me up?" Jane was slightly cross that she had been left out of this adventure.

"Sorry, it was just too dangerous."

"And Twilly's been in the Norahs all along! How did she know you wouldn't give her away?"

"She took a very big risk. She said she just had an instinct that I was prime Norah material — wasn't that nice of her?" Jane had never seen Staffa so lively. "Twilly's really a remarkable person. You should have seen how quickly she told me about the gossip at the race course!"

"Eh? What gossip?"

"I can't explain here. Come into the kitchen."

Staffa grabbed Jane's hand, and dragged her through a door. Jane found herself in a snug kitchen, filled with golden candlelight.

"Your Janeship!" Twilly, half laughing and half crying, flung herself at Jane and hugged her hard. "Did they hurt you? Oh, I'm so glad we got you in time!"

"Twilly!" It was so great to see her other friend that Jane almost felt happy. She sat down on a kitchen chair, and Twilly made three delicious cups of hot dandelion seed tea.

"We can't stay here very long," Staffa said. "Twilly, are her clothes ready?"

Now that there was light, Jane saw that Staffa had taken off the stiff green dress she had worn at the Races and changed into a boy's jacket and pants. Twilly handed a similar outfit to Jane, and the three of them giggled when she put Jane's awful Bo Peep dress on the fire. The new clothes were soft and very comfortable.

"Right," Staffa said, sitting down at the table. "I'll try to explain. Feel free to ask questions."

Jane had so many questions that she hardly knew where to begin. "Why did the queen send Quarley to prison?"

Staffa's strange white skin seemed to harden. "Because he refused to marry the bride she chose for him."

"She can't order him to fall in love," Twilly said, shaking her curls. "Certainly not when he's so dreadfully sad about the old princess!"

"Quarley's always sad," Jane said, thinking about the melancholy young king. "I know the old princess was your granny — but why is he taking it so badly?"

Staffa and Twilly gave each other odd looks.

Staffa said, "That's just it. The old princess wasn't our grandmother. She was Quarley's wife."

THE CHOSEN BRIDE

"HIS *WIFE*?" JANE NEARLY FELL OFF HER CHAIR. STAFFA must have gone crazy. Did she really expect her to believe that the frail old lady had been the wife of the young king?

Staffa said, "I told you, we're not human. We mature more slowly than humans, and we live a lot longer. In your human years, Quarley is nearly a hundred and seventy."

"You're crazy," Jane said. She felt cold.

"I'm afraid not."

"How . . . how old are you, then?"

Staffa said. "I was pretending to be a child of your age

when I was in your world, because that's how I appear to humans. I'm actually sixty-five." She smiled, rather sadly, at Jane's astonishment. "I wasn't very good at being a child, was I? But I hadn't visited your world since 1951, and I was woefully out of date. Hence the antiquated clothes."

"Why did you come to Lower Lumpton?"

"Mother picked your area for the scenery, and the high number of gourmet food shops."

"What were you doing at my school?"

"I wanted to find a friend," Staffa said simply. "You and Twilly are so lucky — you come from lovely big families, and you're allowed to meet people. I never met anyone, because Mother wouldn't let me mix with the Eckers. You can't imagine the loneliness."

"Never mind," Twilly said consolingly. "You've got us now."

"Yes, and it's the best thing that ever happened to me." Staffa was fierce. "I'm never going back to that princess life! Never, ever! I don't care if I starve!"

"You can come back home with me," Jane said hopefully. "The boys would love it."

"Or you can stay here," said Twilly. "Dad can always use an extra pair of hands in the tannery."

"Thanks," Staffa said, smiling. "But I'm forgetting

about the story — please listen to it carefully, Jane. Then you'll understand that none of this is really my fault. You see, all I knew was that Mother was coming to your world on one of her shopping trips. She does this once a year, but she hasn't taken me with her since we visited the Festival of Britain in 1951."

Jane asked, "Why not?"

"I spoke to another child," Staffa said crisply, "and bought her a toffee apple. Mother had me whipped for disobedience."

"She's such a cow!" Jane cried.

Twilly asked, "What's a cow?"

"Well, I suppose it's a bit like one of your slugs, only much more bony — "

"We're getting away from the story again," Staffa said. "This summer, Mother suddenly announced that she was taking me back to your world — and this time, she actually wanted me to make a friend. I was astonished — but SO excited, because this was my dream come true!" She let out a long sigh. "And that's why I wasn't as suspicious as I should have been. I should have known she'd be up to something."

"What?" Jane was trying hard to follow this.

"As I've told you, we're not human in my family. But we

have to marry humans, or our race will die out. So when we want to get married, we come through the box into your world, to find a human mate. Quarley came through in what you would call the 1920s. He met Norah and fell in love." Staffa looked hard at Jane. "She loved him so much that she agreed to follow him into the box and never see Pangbourne again. Norah chose to come here."

She seemed to expect an answer. Jane said, "Oh."

"She was a beautiful girl of twenty." Staffa's eyes filled with tears. "And they were very happy for the first forty years or so — though they never managed to have any children, and Mother was fiendishly jealous. The people loved Norah, you see. And some of them began to ask why the king's wife was only a princess, when she should have been the queen. Well, I daresay you can imagine how furious that made Mother." She added, "Are you following so far?"

"I think so," Jane said. "But I don't see what it's got to do with me."

"I'm coming to that. Poor Norah gradually got older and older, while Quarley stayed young. He had to watch the woman he loved turn into a withered old lady. Mother said she was an embarrassment, and she wanted Quarley to send her away to the hunting lodge and find another wife — but he wouldn't hear of it. He said his heart was broken, and that marrying humans was cruel, and he was never doing it again."

"I bet the queen was angry," Jane said.

"She certainly was." Staffa frowned. "Our human connections are the key to our power over the Eckers. They're waiting for our royal line to end. If there's no new human bride lined up, the Eckers will refuse to be ruled by us."

"Why can't he just marry an Ecker woman?"

Staffa said, "Because Mother would kill him."

"Oh, but — "

"Jane, she really would kill him. Please believe me." Staffa frowned again, and two tears crept down her cheeks. "He's in terrible danger. I'm scared I'll never see him again."

Twilly gave her hand a friendly squeeze. "Cheer up — the Norahs will find a way to save him."

Jane asked, "Won't the Norahs try to kill him too?"

"Oh, no," Twilly said, "the king's been a member for ages. He wants us Eckers to have a proper parliament, and votes, and all sorts of posh things. He's just as sick of the queen as the rest of us."

Staffa sniffed. "Anyway, there was the old princess getting older and older, and the Eckers were getting more and more restless, so Mother took matters into her own hands.

As I've said, it's impossible to bring a human through the box unless they choose to come — of their own free will."

"Like I did," said Jane.

"Yes, Jane. Like you."

They were all quiet for a few minutes. Jane shivered, sensing the approach of something fearful, like an iceberg in an icy sea.

"Every time Mother went into your world," Staffa said, "she tried to find a bride for Quarley, and to bring her through the box. But of course, she could never get anyone to agree — people just thought she was insane. So she decided to use me as bait."

"You? What d'you mean?"

"Oh, Jane! Don't you see? She told me I could find a friend and bring her home for a visit. Please don't be angry — I really, truly didn't know it was a trick!"

Jane's mouth was dry. "A trick?"

"Do you remember that night when her hat was on fire?"

"Yes."

"She'd been back through the box to put down yet another revolution — and she announced that she was bringing back a new human to be the next royal bride."

"But who?"

There was another silence.

In a small voice, Staffa said, "You."

"ME?" choked Jane. "But how can it be me? I'm not old enough to get married!"

"You're the official princess-in-waiting," Staffa said. "She's told everyone that you'll marry Quarley as soon as you're eighteen."

"That's why everyone was staring at you when we went to the Races," Twilly explained breathlessly. "I heard them talking about it. And I heard that you were being sent to the hunting lodge — in case you escaped, or got killed by the Sticks of Darkness. That's why we had to kidnap you in such a hurry."

"The Sticks of Darkness are the anti-royalist group," Staffa said. "They want to kill us all." Her lips trembled. She gulped back a sob. "I know I've got you into a terrible mess, but please don't hate me!"

Jane was in a daze. The queen wanted to put her in prison for seven years and then force her to marry Quarley. There was nothing the matter with Quarley, but that was not the point. The queen meant to trap her in the box forever — until she withered and died like the old princess. If her evil plan succeeded, Jane would never see the Boy Garden again.

She stood up. This was so deeply scary that she was not scared. There was a still, hard anger inside her that made her feel very brave. "I don't want to get married. I want to go home."

Staffa and Twilly looked at each other nervously.

Jane stamped her foot. "Get me home!"

Staffa said, "It's not as simple as that."

"I don't care!" shouted Jane. "I want to go home!"

"Listen to me," Staffa said. "I'll do everything I can to get you home. But until we destroy my mother's power, it's totally impossible."

Jane tried to calm herself down by taking a few deep breaths. "All right," she said. "Let me help you to destroy her. Let me join the Norahs."

"But it could be so dangerous!"

"I don't care! What've I got to lose?"

Before Staffa could argue any more, there was a knock at the door, in rhythm — *rat-tat-TAT*.

Twilly called, "Brown bread!"

A voice outside gasped, "Snail butter!"

The door of the kitchen opened, and Narcas whisked into the room, followed by two middle-aged Eckers. They were all out of breath.

"It's all gone wrong!" panted Narcas. "Oh, what shall we do? Gad's been arrested — now there's nobody to rescue the king! We'll have to call off the revolution and make for the hills!" She collapsed into a chair and buried her face in her hands.

Twilly and Staffa stared at each other in dismay.

The older Eckers, however, were calm.

"No use panicking," said the man. "We'll just have to think again." He had bedspring curls of hair around a large bald patch.

"Well, so this is the human bride," said the woman whose bright, round eyes were just like Twilly's. "Nice to meet you, dearie." She smiled at Jane.

"This is our mam and dad," Twilly told her. "They were supposed to be arranging your next hiding place — "

"We were going to smuggle you out in a bakery van," Narcas said. "But there are double guards on all the city gates. They're looking for you all over the city. The queen's offered a pound of chocolate as a reward for capturing you!"

"And Gad was going to rescue the king," Mam said, still calm. "And the whole revolution was all arranged, as neat as you like. But Gad can't do much in a castle dungeon."

"Yes, it was a bit of a setback," Dad agreed. "How can we get the king now? That's the big question."

Narcas groaned. "It's impossible!"

"No, it isn't!" Staffa cried, very white and determined.

"I refuse to give up now! I'm going to rescue my brother and send Jane home if it kills me!"

Dad shook his head. "It's too dangerous for a little thing like you. Why, you're not seventy!" (If she hadn't been so worried, this would have made Jane smile.)

"I don't care," Staffa said. "I brought Jane here, and she's my responsibility."

Twilly and her parents exchanged troubled looks.

Mam patted Jane's shoulder. "You mustn't worry if we can't break the spell, Miss Jane. You can stay here with me. I'll apprentice you, and you'll grow up to marry a nice young sugarsmith and have your own little shop on Fondant Lane!"

Jane swallowed hard. Mam meant to be comforting, but the idea of spending the rest of her life inside the box was heartbreaking. Meeting Twilly's parents made her think of her own, and she wanted them so much that she could have cried. But this was no time to cry.

"I'm not scared," she said (trying not to sound it). "Let's make a plan!"

Narcas let out another groan. "But it's impossible — unless one of you can ride a bee."

"Oh," said Staffa, turning even paler. "Oh, I hate bees!"

"Gad's a beeman," Dad explained to Jane. "He's engaged to our Pippock, and he flew down this morning under cover of going to the Races. He left his bee in our stable. You see, the mountain fortress is so heavily guarded that a thousand Norahs couldn't get near it — but a single bee might've had a chance."

"I wonder — " Jane said. Everyone turned to her. Her face turned a little hot. "I wonder if it's anything like riding a horse?"

All the Eckers looked blank (horses were quite unknown in this world), so Jane spoke to Staffa. "It's just that I know how to ride a horse — Dad taught us all to ride Leonard. And I wondered if that would be any good with a bee. That's all."

She had half expected them to laugh at her, but they were all very interested.

"It can't be too different," Staffa said slowly. "I mean, bees have reins and saddles, like horses in your world."

Jane's heart began to beat harder. They were taking her seriously, and she wished she hadn't said anything, but her veins fizzed with excitement — how amazing it would be, if she managed to rescue the king!

"Horses don't fly, of course," Staffa went on.

"Oh, I'd forgotten about that," Jane said. "I'm afraid I wouldn't have a clue how to get it off the ground."

Everyone looked disappointed — except Twilly, who gave a little shriek. "Two with your toes!"

Mam shook her head. "What the goodness are you on about?"

Twilly was eager. "Don't you remember what Gad told us? The beemen have that rhyme:

> *Two with your toes*
> *And UP she goes!*
> *Two with your heels,*
> *And DOWN she reels!"*

Once again, everyone looked at Jane. There was no going back now. Two with your toes — well, it was worth a try. She did her best to look brave. "Is there . . . is there somewhere I could practice?"

FATILDA

"I CAN'T LET YOU DO IT!" STAFFA PLEADED. "YOU'LL be shot down — or you'll fall off!"

"It's worth the risk," Jane said.

Dad had led the two of them out into the stable yard at the back of the house. It was dark, but a big, bright moon shone down on the cobblestones, and bathed in silver light the tall bales of slugskin.

The first stall contained a large brown sofa. Dad flashed his lantern at it, and the sofa suddenly stood up on its casters. Jane let out a yelp of shock — it was not a sofa at all, but a huge brown beetle.

"Don't worry," said Dad. "That's just one of my dray beetles that I keep for pulling the cart. They never hurt you unless they sit on you by mistake." He swung his lantern at the next stall. "This is the young lady you've got to watch."

In the soft shadows, the enormous bee looked like a furry helicopter without a propeller. She was covered in thick, shaggy stripes of black and yellow fur. Her six fat, furry legs stamped the floor crossly. Her antennae were curls of metal, like television aerials, and when she turned around, Jane and Staffa shuddered to see her stinger, gleaming poisonously on her fat bottom. Her wings folded and unfolded, and Jane was fascinated to see how neatly the great white fans slotted together.

"Her name's Fatilda," Twilly's dad said in a low, nervous voice. "I think Gad named her after the queen. Look, are you sure about this, Miss Jane? She's ever so vicious! Only Gad can keep her calm."

Jane swallowed, keeping her eyes on the bee. She was very scared, but determined not to show it. "What does Gad do?"

"He talks to her," Dad said. "Soothing like — full of little pet names. He calls her 'blossom' and 'darling' and 'sunbeam.' He's more romantic with that bee than he is with our Pippock!"

Fatilda let out a deep, angry, vibrating buzz so powerful that Jane could feel it in her feet. How was she supposed to call this creature "blossom"? Clenching her fists
to stop herself from trembling, she took a step into
Fatilda's stall.

"Hello, Fatilda," she said. It came out as a squeak. Jane
swallowed again, and did her best to sound soothing. "I
know I'm not your Gad, but I'm on the same side — so I
want you to be a very good girl and let me ride on your
back."

She stopped. The buzzing went on, but the mighty bee
did not seem angry. Jane dared to walk right up to her and
stroke her shaggy sides. It was like patting a great striped
bison. She had a strange smell, partly animal and partly
sugar, as if someone had made hot toffee in the camel
house at the zoo.

"Woah, girl," murmured Jane. Fatilda wore a saddle of
purple slugskin, with oddly shaped silver stirrups. Very,
very cautiously, Jane slipped the purple reins over Fatilda's
head. "Come out now — er — blossom — easy, now!" She
began to lead the bee out into the yard.

Dad and Staffa backed away fearfully. Staffa gasped,
"Be careful!"

Jane took a deep breath. "Fatilda, darling, this is
very important — you're our only hope!" Her mouth was

dry. Could she ever ride this beast? Fatilda was three times the size of dear old Leonard, and at least three times angrier.

"Bees are ever so sensitive," Dad said. "I could swear she knows that something's happened to Gad. She's worried about him."

"Poor thing!" For the first time, Jane felt sorry for the giant bee. "Poor old Fatilda! We'll find your Gad!"

"Oh, stop patting her!" Staffa cried. "She'll kill you!"

"No, she won't — will you, darling?"

Staffa and Dad were still hanging back, but Jane suddenly knew that she could handle Fatilda.

"I'm going to try riding her," she told Dad. "Help me into the saddle."

"I don't know, Miss Jane — I've never been near a bee in my life! But if a little human can risk it — " With a shaking hand, he took Fatilda's reins and led her to some wooden steps on the other side of the yard.

"I can't look!" moaned Staffa. "You'll be killed!"

"If we scare her, she'll sting!" Dad said, his face pale and sweating with fear. "Then you'll drop dead — and so will she! And there'll be nobody to rescue the king!"

It was odd to remember that Fatilda was just like a tiny

bee at home, and would die if she unleashed her deadly poison. But this was life or death, and Jane knew that she had to be brave — the whole country was depending on her. Very nervous, but also excited, she climbed the steps and put one leg over Fatilda's wide, hard back. She stuck her feet into the stirrups. Good grief, she was sitting on the back of a bee!

Staffa asked, "Are you all right? How does it feel?"

"Fine," Jane said. "It's nice being so high up. Pass me the reins."

Dad gave Jane the reins and immediately backed away.

"I'll just walk her for a bit," Jane said. She tried to imagine that she was riding Leonard — and was thrilled to find that riding a bee really was quite a lot like riding a horse. Fatilda was testy, but she was perfectly trained and very obedient.

"I'm going to try flying her now," Jane said. "Stand back!"

She whispered the rhyme to herself. "Two with your toes, and UP she goes!"

She gave two sharp jabs with her toes. Fatilda's buzz became harder and louder. Her wings suddenly shot open, like the tails of peacocks.

The yard fell away beneath them. Incredibly — amazingly — they were flying. Jane guided Fatilda around in a slow circle. This was easy, and it was amazing. It was more than that. It was, Jane decided, the *most* amazing thing that had ever happened to her. Oh, if only they could have huge bees at the Boy Garden. What wonderful battles they could have in the paddock!

"Two with your heels," she muttered. "Come on, Miss Fatilda — let's see if I can land you."

She jabbed the bee's tough sides twice with her heels, and they sank to the ground with majestic grace. Jane patted the back of Fatilda's furry head, and the buzz deepened to a sleepy drone.

Jane laughed. "I think she's purring! Oh, isn't she sweet?"

"Are you nuts?" Staffa was white as paper. "I can't ride that monster!"

"I'm sorry, Princess," Dad said, "but you'll have to ride her — or how will Miss Jane find her way to the fortress?"

"Suppose Fatilda crashes? Suppose my mother's soldiers shoot her down?" Staffa was almost crying. "Oh, Jane, I'll never forgive myself if anything happens to you!"

Jane was about to say something brave when there was a sudden loud thumping on the door of the house.

A rough voice shouted, "Open up, in the name of the queen! We know you've got the human! Open up!" Dad, Jane and Staffa gaped at one another in horror.

Mam hurried out into the yard with a lantern. "You'll have to go now, my dearies — this very minute! It's our only chance!"

Another voice shouted from behind the gates of the yard, "Open up! We've got you surrounded!"

Dad picked Staffa up like a sack of potatoes and threw her onto Fatilda's back behind Jane. "Good luck, you two. Jane, get up in the air as fast as you can to avoid the bullets!"

"Good luck!" cried Mam. "Take care!"

The soldiers were starting to batter down the gates. In a few moments, they would be swarming all over the yard. It was now or never.

Staffa put her arms tightly (a bit too tightly) around Jane's waist, and hid her face in Jane's shoulder. Jane made the two digs with her toes, and Fatilda shot up into the air — until Mam and Dad and the soldiers and the yard were distant specks, and the whole city was spread out below them.

Jane saw orange flashes of fire, and crowds of people fighting in the narrow streets. She heard bullets singing in the warm night air (luckily not high enough to hit them).

"Staffa!" she called over her shoulder, "you've got to stop being scared. I need you to tell me where we're going!"

"I'm so sorry — " moaned Staffa. "I know I'm being foolish — but I can't bear to look down!"

"You've GOT to look down!" Jane shouted desperately. "You've GOT to stop being scared long enough to rescue Quarley!"

"Yes, you're right."

Jane felt Staffa behind her, taking a deep breath and raising her head from Jane's shoulder. For a few seconds, she swayed alarmingly in the saddle.

She gasped, "Follow the canal — towards the lake."

"Are you okay? You're not going to faint or something, are you?"

"No. I'm fine." Staffa's voice was still shaky, but she sat more steadily, and relaxed her grip on Jane's waist.

Far below them, Jane saw the canal, stretching out in the moonlight like a silver ribbon. She steered Fatilda along its course, and in a few minutes they had left the war-torn city far behind.

JANE WOULD REMEMBER IT AFTERWARDS AS THE MOST magical ride of her life. The summer breezes stroked her face. The moonlit landscape was eerily beautiful. Fatilda hummed serenely. Jane felt that the bee had decided to trust her. They rode over woods and fields and hills. They passed over villages and farmhouses. Every so often, Staffa called directions into her ear.

They were flying towards the mountains. Jane recognised these black shapes as the mountains she had seen on the painted box. The scenery became wilder, and more desolate. A cool wind began to whip around them. Fatilda flew higher and higher, over mountain lakes and snowy crags. The two girls shivered with cold.

At last, they saw it — a black fortress built into the rock, with tiny lights blinking in its towers like mean little eyes. It was a terrible place.

"Mother's so-called hunting lodge," Staffa said.

Jane pulled the reins so that Fatilda hovered in midair (this was an odd and not unpleasant feeling, like sitting on a stationary lawn mower). "What do we do now? How do we get inside?"

"We don't," Staffa said. "There are too many guards.

I'm afraid we have to fly around the tops of the towers to find Quarley — without being seen. "

"But that's impossible! Oh, all right — at least we can die trying!" Jane nudged Fatilda with her toes. The bee rose higher in the air, and they sailed over the top of the great black fortress.

As slowly and quietly as possible, they rode around the high, bleak towers, daring to look in at every lighted window. They glimpsed some very awful things — rooms stacked with skeletons, rooms filled with evil-looking knives and guns, a prisoner being whipped. They also saw a card game and some sort of dancing lesson, but there was not a sign of Quarley.

Staffa was worried. "I do hope Mother hasn't sent him somewhere else! I don't think she'll have killed him yet — but you never can tell with Mother."

Finally, at the very top of the highest tower, they looked in at a window, and Jane gasped, "There!"

She reined in Fatilda. There was the young king. He was sitting at a wooden table, reading a book by the light of a candle. There was a large metal collar around his neck.

Staffa hissed, "Quarley!"

Quarley nearly jumped out of his skin, but he had the

sense not to make any noise. He crept across the room to-wards them. "Staffa! Jane! What's going on? Where's the man from the Norahs?"

"Hi Quarley," whispered Jane. "Never mind about all that — someone's going to spot us in a minute. You'd better climb out of the window. I'll try to hold her steady."

He shook his head. "I can't — Mother had me chained to the wall." (Jane saw now that he was holding up a thick metal chain, to prevent it from dragging on the floor and making a noise.) "You'll have to get the keys from the guard!"

"Where is he?"

"On his break," Quarley said, "in the Guards' Social Club, at the very bottom of this tower."

Fatilda was getting restless. Jane stroked her head more firmly. "Easy, Fatty!"

Staffa asked, "How do we recognize your guard?"

"His name's Speevens, and he has a long red beard, which he wears in two braids. The keys will be hanging in a bunch on his back pocket — but it's too dangerous!"

"I think it's a bit late to worry about that," Staffa said grimly. "Let's get down there, Jane. We can work out what to do when we're there."

Jane made the two digs with her heels, and Fatilda plummeted towards the ground so suddenly that Jane's stomach had that left-behind feeling you get in elevators. They landed in a dark yard, closely shuttered, with one small door in the stone wall. Jane and Staffa slid to the ground.

"Ouch!" Jane whispered. "My legs are so stiff!"

She hitched Fatilda to one of the shutters and noticed that her buzz had begun to sputter, like a faulty engine.

"She's tired," Jane said. "It'll do her good to rest for a minute." As if she had understood, Fatilda folded her wings in tightly and toned her buzz down to a sleepy murmur.

From behind the door in the stone wall, they could hear shouts and bursts of laughter and glasses clinking, and — more distantly — the sound of singing. Jane suddenly thought of the pub at home, where Dad worked, and swallowed a pang of homesickness so strong that it almost made her dizzy. She had to forget about home, and concentrate on finding Quarley's guard.

She grabbed Staffa's cold hand. "Come on!"

They ran across the yard, and opened the heavy wooden door a couple of inches. There was nothing on the other side except an empty corridor. The two girls crept inside. Two doors stood open. The pub noises, and the singing, were louder now.

Jane dared to look through the nearest door. She saw a big, smoky room full of guards in black uniforms. They sat around rough wooden tables, and serving maids brought them plates of food and big mugs of foaming stuff that looked a little like beer.

"This is impossible!" Staffa whispered crossly. "There's dozens of them!"

Jane whispered, "Just concentrate on the ones with beards."

There were several men with red beards, and one man with a braided beard, but no one with both. Quickly, knowing that time was running out, Jane and Staffa peeped into the room next door — the room with the singing. A notice on the door said: CHOIR PRACTICE IN PROGRESS.

The choir, all prison guards, sat in a group holding their music books. They were singing a song that Jane had heard before.

"The Ballad of Batsindo!" whispered Staffa.

"And he fell down the plughole — so hairy and wide!" roared the choir.

"STOP!" screeched the conductor. "This is supposed

to be SAD! Tenors, where were you? Start again, from the top of verse nineteen!"

"Look!" Staffa suddenly nudged Jane. "In the middle of the front row!"

It had to be Speevens. His beard was redder than Jane's hair, and woven into two long braids. He was singing very loudly and seriously.

"I think I can see his keys," whispered Jane. "What do we do now?"

Staffa frowned. "We can't do anything now — it would be sheer madness. We'll simply have to wait until this choir practice is over, and follow him. Two of us should be able to handle him."

"He's very big," Jane said doubtfully. "Should we get heavy candlesticks or something, like people do in the movies?"

"Candlesticks? Whatever for?"

"Well — to hit him over the head."

"But he's too tall! We won't be able to reach his head!"

Both of them broke into nervous giggles. Jane had to bite the insides of her cheeks to shut herself up. This kind of illegal laughing is amazingly hard to stop, even when you know that it will get you into trouble.

"This is what we'll do," Staffa said, in a low and steady voice. "Are you listening?"

Jane nodded.

"I can see a flight of stairs — through that little archway thing at the end of this corridor. There appears to be a sort of cupboard under the stairs. We might be able to hide there."

Jane whispered, "What if it's locked?"

"My dear Jane," Staffa said, "I am quite prepared to kill anyone who gets in my way. Do you really think I'd worry about breaking a lock?"

"N-no — "

"Come on!" Staffa pulled her towards the archway, and the shadowy flight of spiral stairs. As Staffa had seen, there was a cupboard at the foot of these stairs. It was not locked. Staffa and Jane hastily bundled themselves into a tiny, damp-smelling space. Staffa kept the door open a crack so that she could watch for Speevens when the choir practice was over.

The singing went on for about another ten minutes, which seemed like ages to the two girls. The cupboard was full of mops and buckets. They sat down on two upturned buckets.

Jane asked, "Would you really kill someone?"

"Only if I absolutely had to," Staffa said. "But I'm not like Mother — I wouldn't do it for fun."

Jane was very afraid. She didn't think she had ever been so afraid in her life. She whispered, "Will we have to kill that Speevens man?"

In the dusty darkness, Staffa felt for Jane's hand, and gave it a reassuring squeeze. "Of course not. Do you remember that day at the Boy Garden, when we ambushed Jon?"

"Yes." Jane winced with homesickness. "The day he stole my chewing gum. We put my hoodie over his head and wrestled him to the ground — What're you doing?"

"Taking off my jacket," Staffa said. "Because we're going to do exactly the same thing to Mr. Speevens. We got the chewing gum, and we'll get those keys. We make a great team, you and I."

Jane immediately felt warmer, and braver. It was true, she thought — she and Staffa made a fantastic team. And if Staffa could keep a cool head, so could she.

The singing stopped. Distantly, they heard the conductor saying, "Thank you, everyone. Same time tomorrow!" And the choir practice was over. Staffa put her eye to the crack in the door, to watch for the braided red beard of Quarley's jailer.

Jane waited impatiently — suppose Staffa missed him in the crowd? She heard the voices and trampling feet of guards passing them in the corridor.

"Here he comes!" hissed Staffa. "He's coming right this way!"

They heard him pause beside the door. They heard his feet climbing the stairs above them, and the ringing of his keys.

"Ready?" whispered Staffa.

"Ready!" whispered Jane.

As quietly and quickly as they could, they ran after Speevens. Staffa threw her jacket over his head, and the tall guard was so shocked that he fell over — just as Jon had done on the day of the chewing gum. Staffa tied his arms, using both their belts (which made Jane's trousers feel rather worryingly loose). Speevens was too dazed to do more than moan, and Jane was rather glad — she didn't really fancy knocking anyone unconscious.

"I've got them!" Staffa waved the bunch of keys. "Back to Fatilda!"

Jane had never run so fast in her life. With her heart in her mouth, she pelted down the winding stairs and along the shadowy corridor, past the door of the guards' pub and out into the yard.

Fatilda lay on the cobbles, a sleeping velvet hump.

"Quick!" Jane said. "Jump on her back while she's crouching!"

Staffa was still not sure about Fatilda. "She's not going to like being woken up!"

The two girls scrambled onto the back of the slumbering bee. Jane saw that the rest had done Fatilda good — she woke with a loud, healthy buzz and flew into the air at the lightest touch of Jane's toes.

Quarley was waiting at the window of his cell. When he saw them, he gasped with relief. "I was sure you'd been caught! What held you up?"

"Choir practice," said Staffa. "I'm throwing in the keys."

She threw the keys through the window. Jane, working to keep Fatilda steady, saw Quarley take the keys to the table, to look at them by the light of the candle. She wanted to snap at him to hurry — he was being pretty casual about this, when their lives were hanging in the balance — but he went on calmly searching through the bunch of keys.

"Girls," he said, "you're both heroines! But why have they sent you into such danger? Where's Gad?"

"Gad's been arrested," Staffa said. "Jane was the only one who could ride a bee."

Quarley laughed softly. "When I saw you two out there, I nearly had a heart attack!" He did not look sad anymore, but full of energy and excitement. "Got it!" He unlocked his metal collar and sprang across to the window. "I'll take the bee from here. We're going to the bee farm. You two get behind me, and hold on as tight as you can — we'll be riding like the wind!"

THE BEE FARM

THIS TIME, THE BEEBACK RIDE WAS NOT SO PLEASANT. Quarley rode Fatilda very fast, through bitter winds, over a stony wasteland. Jane's hands, clutching the back of Quarley's belt, became numb with cold. She was very tired, and very hungry, and her legs were sore with the effort of staying upright in the saddle.

Fatilda suddenly dived down towards a cluster of lights. Jane saw a high fence, and big buildings like aircraft hangars.

Quarley jumped down briskly and helped down the two girls. He tied Fatilda to a wooden post. Jane's legs were so stiff that she could hardly walk.

"It's the king!" a shrill voice cried. "Hurrah! They've done it!" Light poured out of an open door. "Come in out of this wind!"

"Hello, Pippock," said Quarley. "How are you?"

The sister of Twilly and Narcas bustled out to meet them — this was the sister who worked as the bee farm cook and was engaged to the owner of Fatilda. Pippock's hair was in neat curls under a snow-white cap. She was a very neat person and looked a lot like Mam.

"Oh, Your Majesty — we're all in an uproar! Narcas sent a post fly to warn us! They've all been taken to prison — Mam and Dad and Narcas, and my poor Gad!"

"Take courage," said Quarley. "It won't be for long. Can you give these girls something to eat?"

Pippock darted forward to kiss Jane and Staffa. "You poor little dears — come inside this minute!"

She took them into a canteen, full of long tables and benches. It was beautifully warm, and amazingly clean. The walls were covered with strict notices — NO BOOTS! TOOLS TO BE LEFT OUTSIDE! UNWASHED HANDS WILL BE SLAPPED! — and Pippock made the king wipe his feet twice. Jane remembered Twilly saying that she was rather bossy.

A big pan of greenfly soup bubbled above the blazing kitchen fire. The smell made Jane's stomach rumble.

Pippock served them each a steaming bowlful. It tasted delicious.

"Phew, that's better," Quarley said. "You can't imagine the stuff I've been eating in prison. I hope you're not too tired, girls."

"I'm not tired at all, now that I've had something to eat," Jane said. "What happens next?"

Staffa asked, "When do we overthrow Mother?"

"All in good time. There's something I have to do first." To their surprise, Quarley grinned at Pippock. "Is everything ready?"

She giggled back at him. "Yes, Your Majesty. They're all waiting in Hive One."

He stood up. "Come along, you two — I want you to watch this."

Pippock suddenly shrieked, "Wait!" She pounced on the king and pinned a large white flower to his uniform. "Oh, I do hope I don't cry!"

What was going on? Jane looked at Staffa, but Staffa was obviously as puzzled as she was.

They left the warm canteen and crossed a dark, windy yard. Quarley opened a small door in one of the huge hangars.

The inside of the beehive was one of the most incredible sights Jane had ever seen. One whole wall looked, at first, like a very dingy aquarium — but when you looked properly, it was rows and rows of wax cells. The wax was like thick and dirty glass. Inside each cell, you could see the dark shape of an enormous bee. The air was warm and damp. There was a loud, low buzzing noise, which made the floor shake, and a strong smell of honey. Jane could not see the special cell that belonged to the majestic queen bee, but it was the invisible center here, like the engine room on a ship.

A great crowd of beemen waited for them. All the men were armed with the big tools of their dangerous trade — some with honey paddles, some with comb shears and some with wax knives. Their weapons gleamed in the dim light, and they looked very fierce. When they saw Quarley, they burst into loud cheers. "Long live the king! Power to the Norahs!"

"Thank you," said Quarley. "My mother's reign is nearly over. But first, the ceremony!"

The crowd of beemen parted. Staffa and Jane gasped.

There, on the sticky floor of the great hive, stood a small figure all dressed in white, her face hidden by a white veil.

"My bride," said Quarley.

Pippock wiped her eyes. "Oh, doesn't she look lovely? I knew I'd cry!"

Jane and Staffa stared — this was the last thing they had expected.

"Your — *bride*?" whispered Staffa. "I don't understand!"

Quarley lowered his voice. "I know I've only just lost poor Norah, and I'd hate you to think I'm not sorry — but she knew I loved Migorn, and she gave us her blessing. Please believe me, Staffa. She even left us her human kettle as a wedding present!"

"That's not what I meant," Staffa said. "Mother will go crazy!"

"Mother's not in charge anymore," Quarley said cheerfully. "Don't you see? This ruins all her plans — she can't force poor Jane to marry me if I'm married already!"

He took his place beside the bride. She threw back her veil, revealing golden curls and a beautiful Ecker face — a very famous face.

Jane cried, "Migorn! He's marrying Migorn! Now I understand that play!"

Pippock blew her nose. "Yes, and after the revolution she'll be our very first Ecker queen! Isn't it romantic?"

"But . . . but . . ." Staffa was too amazed to speak.

"We've been going out together for ages," Quarley explained. "Sorry I couldn't tell you before, but it would have been too dangerous — Mother would have killed her. I hope you're not shocked."

"Oh!" Staffa said. "This is — wonderful!" She started to laugh, and then started to cry, and had to borrow Pippock's handkerchief.

An old man with a gray beard came out of the crowd and stood before the young couple. Jane wondered if he was a vicar. Did they have vicars in this world?

"Migorn," said the old man, "do you take this man to be your lawful husband?"

"I do!" said Migorn.

"Quarles, do you take this woman to be your lawful wife?"

"I do!" said Quarley.

"With the power vested in me as controller of Bee Farm Forty-nine in the Sackenwald District," said the old man, "I pronounce you man and wife." (The controller of the farm was obviously qualified to marry people, like a ship's captain in our world).

Everyone in the beehive bowed low.

"Three cheers for the new queen!" yelled Pippock.

The cheers were so deafening that the bees became restless, and began to growl and trample in their waxy cells.

Staffa hugged her brother and shyly kissed Migorn. "Congratulations! This is the best news ever!"

"We're sisters now," Migorn said. "Can we be friends too?"

"I'd love us to be friends," Staffa said, beaming all over her childish face. "And I always wanted a sister!"

Quarley jumped up on top of a honey barrel. "Comrades!" he shouted. "Are you with me?"

"YES!" roared the beemen.

Suddenly, everyone was running — Jane was nearly knocked over in the rush. Staffa and Migorn pulled her into the shelter of the wall, and she watched in amazement.

A group of beemen pushed open two immense doors. The other beemen were running up a series of ladders that crisscrossed the wax cells. Each man cut his way into a cell and mounted a bee. In a moment, the hive was a mass of angry bees, streaming through the doors into the night air.

"Don't dawdle, Miss Jane!" Pippock grabbed her hand. "It's time to climb aboard that bee of yours — forgive me for crying, but she reminds me of my poor Gad! Oh, I hate to think of that angel of a man, locked up in a cold dungeon!"

Ducking their heads under the flying bees, the girls made their way outside. Fatilda was waiting for them. Jane's spirits lifted — she was sure Fatilda was pleased to see her. The touchy bee stopped whining and kicking and began to make her purring noise. Jane stroked her neck. She hadn't thought it was possible to be fond of a particular, individual bee (in our world it would be considered very odd), but she did feel fond of Fatilda, and it somehow made her extra confident.

She gave her a hard hug, and murmured in what might have been her ear, "I'm pleased to see you, too!"

It was a magnificent sight. Several hundred bees flew in tight formation, led by Quarley on a beautiful, trained queen. The three girls rode in the middle of the group on Fatilda, surrounded by an armed guard. The massed bees of Farm 49 were joined by hundreds — thousands — of bees from other farms nearby. Together, in a great humming swarm, they flew towards the city.

"This is incredible!" Jane said over her shoulder to Staffa. "When we swoop down, they won't have a chance!"

This was the plan — a surprise attack from the air.

Staffa was still worried. "Mother won't go quietly. If she wins, her revenge will be horrible. She never forgives."

"Oh, I know her sort!" Migorn said darkly. "I was in the chorus with someone just like her."

Migorn, when you got to know her, was a nice girl — cheerful and brave, and tougher than she had looked onstage. She passed Jane and Staffa little hard sweets that tasted of soap, and playfully threw sweets at the bodyguards, and made all kinds of rude jokes about the queen. But her senses stayed pin sharp, and she was one of the first to hear the new and sinister noise above the hum of the bees.

She hissed, "Listen!"

It was a harsh, ugly, droning noise — very distant, but steadily getting louder.

Jane asked, "Is that thunder, or something?"

"We're under attack!" yelled one of the bodyguards. "It's the Wasp Squad!"

Suddenly, the dark sky above them was filled with black shapes — winged shapes, with multiple stings glinting evilly in their tails, ridden by the queen's most murderous soldiers. The three girls screamed and clung together while an aerial battle raged around them. The huge wasps roared down upon the king's air force. Bees and men dropped from the sky. Jane saw Quarley on his trained queen, desperately fighting off two of the hideous creatures. Wasps were bad enough, Jane thought, when they ruined picnics at home. In this world, where they were the size of small planes, they were spine-chilling. These were not homely, domestic beasts, like Fatilda, but ruthless fighting machines. When you saw them close up, their black-and-yellow bodies had a greasy sheen, and their heads were mean and pointed.

"Jane, she mustn't catch you!" Staffa cried. "She'll send you to prison — and she'll kill Migorn — if the wasps don't kill her first!"

"Let's make a break for it!" Jane shouted — struggling to keep the terrified Fatilda under control.

"But where can we go?"

Migorn was calm. "Follow my directions, Jane — I know a place in the city where they'll hide us."

THE DIAMOND SAW

FATILDA ZOOMED AWAY FROM THE CHAOS OF THE battle so fast that the three girls had to cling to her back for dear life.

"We've done it!" gasped Migorn. "We've shaken them off! Keep her flying low, Jane — and make for the city!"

The first gray streaks of morning had appeared in the sky. Jane saw the roofs and towers of the city ahead of them. As soon as they reached the outskirts, they could see fighting in the streets below.

"See that pink house ahead?" Migorn said in Jane's ear. "Try to land in the yard!"

It was now light enough for Jane to see a big, square, pink house, set in the middle of a large yard. She dug in her heels and pulled the reins, and the exhausted bee landed gently on the lawn.

Jane gave Fatilda a hug, and stroked her head in the way she seemed to like so much. "Good girl! You're a heroine!"

The three of them dismounted. It was odd, after the scary ride, to find themselves standing in a quiet suburban garden, among shrubberies and flowerbeds. But they could hear shouts and gunshots in the street outside. They were still in danger.

"Let's hide her in the forget-me-nots," said Migorn. She helped Jane to guide Fatilda into the shelter of the bushes.

Jane took a good look at the pink house. There was a large sign above the front door: NORAH HALL — HOME OF THE FAMOUS DANCING ORPHANS.

"This is where I grew up," Migorn explained. "I was a Dancing Orphan — that's how I started in the theater business. I know they'll never betray us!"

She knocked on the door.

"Go away!" shouted a quavery voice inside. "I warn you, this house is full of brutal men — all armed to the teeth and completely without mercy!"

Migorn bent down and called through the letterbox, "Miss Dizzy, please let us in! It's Migorn! We're hiding from the queen!"

"Migorn! My dear child!" The front door opened, to reveal an old Ecker lady with her gray hair in curlers, wearing a dressing gown and clutching a rolling pin. "Come in at once!"

Jane and Staffa found themselves in a big hall, with a painting of the old princess smiling above the fireplace. If they hadn't been in danger, Jane might have smiled — the "brutal men" turned out to be several dozen frightened little girls, armed with forks, spoons, egg whisks and brooms.

When they saw Migorn, the little girls dropped these improvised weapons, and crowded around her with cries of joy. She hugged and kissed them as if they had been her sisters, and gave the biggest hug to Miss Dizzy. "I knew you'd help us!"

"Good gracious!" cried Miss Dizzy. "You've brought Princess Staffa — and the human bride!" She understood the danger at once. "Dear me, where can we hide you? The queen's soldiers are swarming all over the neighborhood!"

"The attics!" suggested Migorn.

"The cellar!" cried one of the Dancing Orphans.

"Too obvious," said Miss Dizzy. "I know a far better place — girls, pick up your weapons!"

"Yes, Miss Dizzy!" chorused the orphans.

"Quick as you can, my dears!" The old lady nodded to Migorn, Jane and Staffa, and trotted briskly across the hall. She led them along a corridor, through a back door and across another stretch of lawn. The sun had risen now. In the rosy light of dawn, Jane saw a large wooden building a little like a bandstand in a public park.

"The summer theater," said Migorn. "Of course!"

Miss Dizzy took a big bunch of keys from her pocket. "There's a secret room under the stage. You remember it, Migorn — it's where you used to hold your naughty midnight feasts."

"You knew about the feasts?"

"Don't be silly, dear, of course I knew! That's why the cake tins were always left open." Miss Dizzy unlocked a small wooden door at the side of the building. Jane and Staffa followed Migorn into a dark, damp-smelling space like a cellar. "You can't see the door from the outside. Keep as quiet as possible, and they'll never — "

Miss Dizzy stopped suddenly, and turned pale.

Someone was banging loudly on the front door of the pink house.

A trumpeting voice, horribly familiar, shouted, "Open this door! Give me my human bride!"

"Oh lawks," Staffa said, "Mother! How did she find us?"

"You've been followed," said Miss Dizzy. "I'll hold her off as long as I can!" She hurried out of the secret room, locking the door behind her.

Jane, Staffa and Migorn were left in shaking silence — was there a chance that they could stay hidden?

The voice of the queen was coming across the garden, towards the theater. "I know she's here, Miss Dizzy — I've found the bee she was riding! She's not in the house, so she must be hiding in this shed."

"It's not a shed!" snapped Miss Dizzy. "It's our Summer Pavilion Theater, and we've just had it repainted!"

"Well, you needn't have bothered," said the queen. "The minute the revolution is over, I'm having this orphanage shut down. Dancing Orphans, indeed! Dancing troublemakers, more like!"

"Your Majesty!" begged Miss Dizzy, "they're only little girls! And they have nowhere else to go!"

"They can come and work in my kitchens."

The three girls clutched one another's cold hands. They heard trampling footsteps on the stage, right above their heads.

"Look, I'm on the stage!" boomed the queen. "Friends, Romans and Whatsits — ha ha! What's under here?"

"Nothing!" squeaked Miss Dizzy bravely.

"Oh, NO!" Migorn gasped suddenly. "She's standing on the TRAP DOOR!"

There was a loud crack and a deafening scream, and the queen fell through the trap door into the secret room, narrowly missing Staffa.

"I WISH I'D SQUASHED YOU!" THE QUEEN TOLD STAFFA. "Call yourself a daughter? You're going straight to prison, young lady!"

Staffa, Migorn and Jane were chained to the big fireplace, in the hall of the pink house. Two soldiers with guns stood guard over Miss Dizzy and her orphans. The queen (wearing a ridiculous uniform of purple satin) paced angrily to and fro, eating the orphans' sweets.

"Jane — you'll be going to prison too," the queen went on. "And as for this little hussy — "

"Hussy yourself," Migorn said bravely. "You old bag!"

"Oh, you won't be so insulting when you're living in a cage, Miss Migorn! And you'll be whipped every night, for daring to think you could marry my son! Why, you haven't a drop of human blood!"

"You can't keep me here," Jane said. "I want to go home!"

The queen was calm. "Stop all this fussing, Jane. You are a future princess — many a girl would leap at the chance! One week from today, your parents will receive the sad news of your death."

Jane swallowed hard several times, to stop herself from crying. This was dreadful. In one week, if she didn't escape from this world, poor Mom and Dad would think their only daughter was dead.

"Oh, what a relief," the queen said. "That terrible racket outside has finally stopped!"

Jane and Staffa stared at each other — it was true, the shouts and explosions outside had stopped. There was nothing but silence now, and it grew deeper every minute.

"That means my side has won," the queen said with one of her nasty red smiles. "So we're back to normal — except that I've thought of a few new punishments."

A well-known voice called from outside, "Mother, it's all over! The city has fallen, your soldiers have been defeated, and I'm in charge!"

"It's Quarley!" cried Migorn. "He's won!"

The three girls, the orphans and Miss Dizzy broke into loud cheers.

"AAARGH!" bellowed the queen. Her face turned as purple as her satin uniform. Her soldiers dropped their weapons and put their hands in the air.

One of them mumbled, "I told you we should have joined the other side!"

If Jane hadn't been in chains, she would have jumped up and down with joy. In walked Quarley, with a band of loyal Norahs. The queen's soldiers were tied up and taken away. The girls were released, and Staffa and Migorn rushed to hug the king.

Staffa then flung her arms around Jane. "They did it! They smashed her power! Now I can live with Eckers and everything will be lovely!"

"Curtsey to the true king, girls!" Miss Dizzy cried to the orphans. "And don't take any notice of that old bum in purple!"

One of the orphans asked, "Isn't she still the queen?"

"No, dear," said Miss Dizzy. "Migorn is the queen now. And I expect she'd like you all to dance at her Coronation Ball. I'm taking bookings, Your Majesty!"

All this time, the queen had been huffing and puffing

like a stranded whale. She gave a sudden shriek and jumped to her feet. "SHE will never be queen!"

"Mother," said Quarley, "please don't be a nuisance. Migorn's already the queen — we're married."

"Rubbish!" barked the queen. "It's not legal"

Staffa said, "Why do you have to spoil everything? I think it's lovely!"

"HE'S GOING TO MARRY JANE!" The queen bellowed this so loudly that a thin crack appeared in the ceiling.

"Jane's going home," Quarley said, giving Jane a friendly smile. She smiled back, feeling suddenly very happy. She was going home — to the messy, noisy, grubby, glorious Boy Garden. To Mom, Dad, funny Martin, crazy Dan and Jon, cheeky Mike and Phil, and squirmy little Ted. She wanted them all so much that it hurt.

The queen said, "Jane's not going anywhere — I'm going to keep her here until you change your mind! And there's nothing you can do about it!"

"Mother, please," Quarley said in a patient voice. "Give me the diamond saw."

"NO!"

"Give me the diamond saw, Mother."

"NO! — ha! What're you going to do now? You can't

do a thing without it, but you'll never guess where I've hidden it!"

Jane nudged Staffa. "What's she talking about?"

"It's the key to the spell," Staffa said. She was anxious. "To bring a person into the box, you have to cut off a little piece of their hair with a special tiny saw made of diamond. If you're going back the other way, you need the diamond saw to cut the ring."

Jane looked at the gold ring on her little finger. She had tried many times to pull it off, and it would never budge. It seemed to be fixed deep in her bone.

She asked, "Why didn't she cut off any of my hair?"

"She did," Staffa said. "You must have been asleep, or something."

A memory came back to Jane. She shut her eyes to recapture it. "My dream! It wasn't a dream after all — I thought she was just bending over me, but she was cutting off my hair!" She was so excited that she could hardly get the words out. "And I know where she put the saw! It's up the leg of her bloomers — the left leg!"

"Drat!" swore the queen. She shot out one of her meaty hands, grabbed Migorn and whipped a gleaming dagger out of her purple uniform.

"Let me go!" cried Migorn. She struggled and fought,

but the queen was too strong for her. She held the point of the dagger against Migorn's neck.

"If anyone comes near my bloomers," said the queen, "I'll cut this hussy's horrid Ecker throat!"

Miss Dizzy had a small silver whistle hanging on a chain around her neck. She blew two sharp blasts. In a flash, the Dancing Orphans had leapt across the room and jumped all over the queen.

"Help!" she roared, "Quarley — Staffa — help! They're killing me! Eeek! It tickles! Help!"

As quick as light, the orphans snatched the dagger and saved Migorn. They tied the queen's hands and feet with the pink ribbons from their ballet shoes, until she lay squirming on the floor like a great purple slug.

The smallest orphan went up to Quarley. She curtseyed and held out something small and sharp and very bright.

"Give that back!" yelled the queen, wriggling in her pink ribbons. "You don't know how to use it!"

"The diamond saw!" Quarley exclaimed. "Did you get that?" The little girl nodded shyly, and he bent down to give her a kiss. "Well done!"

Miss Dizzy blew her whistle again. The orphans left the queen and stood in a neat group — like soldiers, but in ballet poses.

Jane, Staffa, Migorn and Quarley all clapped.

"Very nice work, my dears," said Miss Dizzy, her wrinkled old face beaming. "Princess Norah would be proud of you!"

"This country is RUINED!" groaned the queen.

Quarley was trying not to laugh. "Mother, the revolution has happened. There's going to be an election."

"No!"

"The people will elect a proper parliament, and they'll tell me what to do — not the other way around. I'll just sign things and give medals."

"Yuck! That's disgusting!"

"The new age of democracy has begun," said Quarley. "And I really feel you'd be more comfortable in prison."

"I wanted to send you to the fortress," said Staffa. "But Quarley was too kind. He's had the old princess's rooms redecorated. It won't be nearly as bad as you deserve. You'll have plenty of servants to shout at, and all the Haw-haw you can drink."

"You'll go to your rooms immediately," Quarley went on, more sternly. "And in case you have any ideas of escaping, you'll be guarded by one of my best Norahs."

When this guard came into the room, the queen moaned, "ET TU, HOOTER?"

"Yes, madam," said Captain Hooter — for it was none other. "I joined the Norahs in the first week."

The queen was carried out by ten panting soldiers. This time, everybody clapped.

FREEDOM

THE REST OF THAT DAY WAS PURE HAPPINESS AND celebration, and now that Jane knew she was going home, she felt free to enjoy herself. The streets of the city were filled with people singing and dancing, and the gubb stalls were out doing a roaring trade. It was like walking through a fairground.

At the castle, Jane saw soldiers taking down a huge portrait of the queen and replacing it with a handsome picture of Quarley. Someone had drawn a mustache on the face of the queen. Every room that Jane and Staffa went into seemed to have a party going on in it, and they joined in at least six until they got too tired.

"Jane," said Quarley, "I have one more favor to ask. Would you stay here one more day? My wife would like you to be a maid of honor at our coronation."

"Well," Jane said. She was longing to go home. But Staffa and Migorn looked so hopeful, and the coronation sounded so exciting, that she agreed to stay.

She was very glad afterwards, because it turned out to be one of the greatest days of her life. Staffa and Twilly were also maids of honor. They all wore long white dresses with silver sashes, long silver gloves and silver shoes. The king gave them each a beautiful gold medal on a big gold chain.

Jane was very pleased to see Fatilda, in a gold saddle, flying with the Guard of Honor. Staffa was radiantly happy because she was going to a real school for girls. "It's a boarding school in the country, and there'll be loads of other sixty-five-year-olds! I can't wait!"

And Twilly was almost radioactive with happiness because she had landed the job of her dreams. "I can hardly believe it!" she kept saying. "I'm going to be the personal maid of Queen Migorn!"

The coronation took place in the open air, on the castle lawn, and was very magnificent. The king had invited all the bravest Norahs, and Twilly's whole family had places of honor at the front. In the evening, there was a grand

Coronation Ball. Jane knew that she would never see sights like these again — the caged fireflies, the coaches carved from nutshells and drawn by gold-painted beetles, the graceful Dancing Orphans (who performed a new dance called "The Queen Basher," to great applause).

But she was aching to get home, and woke up the next morning full of impatience and anxiety — suppose something went wrong?

Twilly gave her the human clothes she had arrived in. "I didn't really put them in the boiler, Miss Jane, though the queen told me to."

"Thanks!" Jane scrambled into her wonderful, familiar, comfortable human clothes. Now it was time to be human again. Holding Twilly's hand, she went downstairs.

Quarley and Staffa were waiting in the hall of the castle, underneath the huge portrait of Tornado. Quarley carried his mother's silver pickax.

"Are you ready, Jane?"

"Yes."

"I'm afraid it's time to say your good-byes. It's not safe to take these girls any farther."

This was a horrible moment. Jane looked at Staffa and Twilly, and could not bear to think that she would never see them again. They were all crying.

"Good-bye, Twilly!" Jane hugged her. "Thanks for being so kind to me — I'll always be particularly kind to field mice now!"

"Good-bye, Miss Jane!"

They clung together until Quarley gently tapped Jane's shoulder. "I hate to hurry you, but I'm anxious to get this job done as quickly as possible — you'll see why."

Jane untangled herself from Twilly's skinny arms. She looked at Staffa.

"I'm going to miss you, " she mumbled. It seemed like a silly thing to say, when she wanted to say so much more.

Staffa said, "I'm going to miss you, Jane. Give my love to the boys. And to your parents. Please don't forget me. I should like to be remembered sometimes, in your world."

Jane hugged her. "I'll never forget you! And however many friends I make at the new school, there'll never be another friend like you!"

"Good-bye, Jane!" Staffa kissed her and slipped something into the pocket of her jeans.

"What're you doing?"

"It's your coronation medal," Staffa said. "If it's in your pocket when you go through, it'll grow with you. Then you'll have a souvenir."

"Oh — thanks! Good-bye — good-bye, Staffa!"

"Come, Jane," Quarley said, holding out his hand.

Jane sadly turned away from her two friends and took his hand. They walked to the gatehouse of the castle, where she had first entered the box. Beyond the tall gates lay a whitish-bluish swirl of light.

"The light is from your world," Quarley said. "We're at the crossing point."

The big castle gates opened. In walked an elderly pair of Eckers, each carrying a small suitcase.

"Ah, here they are, right on time. Jane, you remember Mr. and Mrs. Prockwald."

"Bless her," said Mrs. Prockwald. "She'd never seen us without our scarves! Hello, dearie. Oh, it's nice to be a decent size again! The king ran down to the farmhouse to fetch us the minute the queen was locked up. Wasn't that nice?"

Her husband said, "Hello, Miss Jane. Nice to see you." He turned to Quarley. "I left the keys in the car, sire. We've brought the little talking thing, just as you instructed. We left it on the ground, a few inches from the box."

"Thanks, you've done very well," said Quarley.

"And there's a box of teabags on the draining board at the farm," said Mrs. Prockwald. "And some nice, nourishing Mars Bars — can't send you home without a healthy meal inside you! Good-bye, dearie!" She gave Jane a smacking kiss. So did Mr. Prockwald. They picked up their suitcases and walked happily away into the castle.

Jane asked, "What're the Prockwalds doing here? Who's at that farm place?"

"Nobody," Quarles said calmly. "I've closed down the farm — we won't be keeping any more of our people in the human world."

"But — how will I get off the island?"

"You'll see. You mustn't be afraid, Jane."

Quarley held her hand tightly. Together they walked through the castle gatehouse and stepped onto the draw-bridge. Jane's stomach turned a somersault. She was a grain of sand in an hourglass, and the hourglass had just been turned over.

Suddenly, there was a new kind of ground beneath her sneakers.

She stopped, trembling. "Is this my world? What's that big silver building over there?"

"It's not a building, it's the cellphone," said Quarley. "Left on the ground by the Prockwalds before they crossed. This is what you will use to get home. I have left a letter for your parents on the kitchen table of the farm, in which I apologize for deserting you on a remote Scottish island."

Jane looked over her shoulder. There was the painted box. It looked rather like a huge movie screen — the painted trees waved, people swarmed around the painted turrets. But it was clear to Jane that she was looking into another dimension.

Quarley kept hold of Jane's hand — the one with the ring. "Keep still, and don't be frightened." He began to saw at Jane's ring with the diamond saw. It seemed to take a long time. When the ring finally sprang apart, Jane saw why it was important to be outside.

She was soaring into the air. The sky rushed to meet her, so fast she was afraid she would bang her head against it. She felt herself screaming, but no sound came out. She was at the center of a great howling, whirling wind.

And then everything was silent — only it was a new kind of silence, one that made Jane's heart leap hopefully. There were no forests of grass, no gigantic insects. She was lying on the bare hillside, and the painted box gleamed between the two boulders.

She was big again! She was back! She wanted to laugh and shriek and turn cartwheels.

Quarley was beside her, brushing dirt from his uniform. He had slipped off his ring, and was now the same size as a normal human. He didn't look quite normal, however — his skin was too hard and too white, and in the common daylight of our world, his hair had a dull, plastic sheen.

He picked up the cellphone. "You will take this phone thing, Jane — which I presume you know how to operate. You will walk to the Prockwalds' farm and telephone your parents. You will then dial nine-nine-nine and ask for the Coast Guard, who will take you off the island. Please help yourself to food and drink while you're waiting to be rescued. And if there's any money left in the car, please keep it. Oh — and don't forget all those new human clothes my mother bought you. They're in two suitcases in the hall. Do you understand so far?"

"Yes."

"Dear Jane, before you leave this place, there is one very important thing you must do for me."

He handed her the queen's silver pickax. Jane staggered under the unexpected weight of it. "When I shrink again," Quarley said, "I want you to count to a thousand. When you have counted, take the silver pickax and smash the box to smithereens. Do you understand?"

"I think so. You're sort of closing the door."

Quarley smiled. "Exactly. It's been a pleasure to know you, Jane." He leaned forward to kiss her cheek.

And he was gone. Jane was alone on the empty hillside, listening to the wind and the cries of the gulls.

SHE DID NOT MOVE FOR A LONG TIME, BECAUSE SHE WAS so afraid of accidentally squashing the king on his journey back to the box. She counted to five thousand, to be extra sure she had given him enough time. Then — looking carefully at the ground with every step — she walked the few yards to the heap of boulders.

She pulled the box out into the open. Its colors were like stained glass with the sun behind it. She stood staring at it for a long time, trying to print the pictures on her memory. It was time to destroy this beautiful thing, so that the kingdom of Eck could shut out the dangerous human world and live in peace. She mustn't worry that she was smashing a world — this was only a meeting point between two worlds.

"Good-bye, box," she said aloud.

She took a mighty swing with the silver pickax. The box splintered into a dozen pieces. She swung the pickax again and again, until it lay in a hundred fragments, scattered across the rough grass like paint-stained matchwood.

Jane tucked the silver pickax under one arm. Just

before she began her walk to the deserted farm, she picked up one painted fragment. Despite all the fear and danger, this had been an incredible vacation. She knew she could never tell anyone about it — her memories of the world inside the box were already fading. There couldn't be any harm in keeping a souvenir.

As she put it in her pocket, she remembered the coronation medal. Her fingers closed on something hard and round, wrapped in a scrap of paper. Jane stared at her gold medal for a long time. It was now about the size of a quarter, on a chain of astonishing, shimmering delicacy. Jane had never owned anything as beautiful as this. She fastened it around her neck.

Then she smoothed out the piece of paper, and saw that Staffa had written something. The letters were a little distorted, but perfectly clear — "Love You Always."

Jane cried a bit at this, yet found it oddly comforting that someone in another dimension would love her always.

The real world rushed to meet her as she walked back to the farmhouse. She was going to have quite a job explaining it all to the Coast Guard — she didn't even know the name of the island she was on. And how on earth were Mom and Dad going to fetch her from the north of Scotland? How could she tell her brothers that they would never be seeing Staffa again?

Not that anything really mattered — it was lovely to have ordinary little worries again. Jane hurried down the steep path on the stony hillside, her long hair whipping in the fresh sea breeze, and there was no happier girl in this or any other world.

Thank you for reading
this FEIWEL AND FRIENDS book.

The Friends who made

THE LITTLE SECRET

possible are:

Jean Feiwel, publisher

Liz Szabla, editor-in-chief

Rich Deas, creative director

Elizabeth Fithian, marketing director

Barbara Grzeslo, associate art director

Holly West, assistant to the publisher

Dave Barrett, managing editor

Nicole Liebowitz Moulaison, production manager

Jessica Tedder, associate editor

Caroline Sun, publicist

Allison Remcheck, editorial assistant

Ksenia Winnicki, marketing assistant

Kathleen Breitenfeld, designer

Find out more about our authors and artists
and our future publishing at
www.feiwelandfriends.com.

OUR BOOKS ARE FRIENDS FOR LIFE